IONA
RISING

BOOK THREE OF THE SYNAXIS CHRONICLES

An Epic Science Fiction Thriller by

Robert David MacNeil

DEDICATION

This book is dedicated to my amazing wife Linda, for her patience and continual encouragement, and for believing this book should be written.

To my friends and family who read the draft version and offered so many great suggestions.

To Lisa and Susan who painstakingly edited the manuscript, correcting my many errors.

And to Keith, whose gift of "second sight" prompted the writing of this book.

Published by Robert David MacNeil

ISBN-13: 978-1543091632
ISBN-10: 1543091636

TABLE OF CONTENTS

PART FOUR: RESCUE MISSION

EPILOGUE

NOTES

ABOUT THE AUTHOR

"There is no question that there is an unseen world. The problem is, how far is it from Midtown and how late is it open?" – Woody Allen (*Without Feathers,* p. 11.)

"There are more things in heaven and earth, Horatio, than are dreamt of in your philosophy." – William Shakespeare (*"Hamlet"*, Act 1 scene 5)

"Our present sufferings are not worth comparing with the glory that will come." – Saul of Tarsus (Romans 8:18)

* * *

With a few minor exceptions, all geographical descriptions in this book are accurate.

All historical references in this book are accurate.

All present-day characters in this book are fictional, and are not intended to represent any persons, living or dead.

The SYNAXIS, of course, is real.

CAST OF CHARACTERS

Lys Johnston – Lys (rhymes with bliss) has the ability to open portals to other worlds. Her gift has taken her to Hell and back to rescue Jamie Thatcher. But who will rescue Lys when Hell comes to earth?

Patrick O'Neil – Patrick is engaged to Lys Johnston. He's faced the possibility of losing Lys once when she went to Hell in an attempt to rescue Jamie, but now, less than a week before their wedding, his fiancée has disappeared.

Roger Johnston – Roger is Lys Johnston's brother. Roger died helping to rescue Jamie Thatcher from Hell, but it now appears that he's come back. But is it really Roger?

Jamie Thatcher – Jamie was rescued from terrible torment in the realm of Hades. Now she must choose to go back.

Marissa Kobani – Marissa was a medical doctor with the World Health Organization, working in the refugee camps of northern Iraq. When she is captured by ISIS, Marissa finds herself in a nightmare beyond her wildest imagining.

The Sheikh – A terrorist mastermind working with the Archons to bring complete destruction to the human race.

Grat Dalton – A psychopath enlisted by the Archons to implement their most horrendous plan yet.

Michael and Erin Fletcher – Michael is an angelologist. Erin heads up the Iona synaxis. To save the world from destruction, Michael must decipher an ancient prophecy and rebuild the ancient monument at Stonehenge.

Derek and Piper Holmes – Founders of the first synaxis, they now travel the world planting new ones in an attempt to thwart the Archon invasion.

The Archons – The Archons are race of malevolent beings from the parallel dimension of Hades. They have great mental powers and are transdimensional—able to move freely between dimensions. Their goal is to destroy the human race and seize our world for their own. Known in human legends as demons, their homeworld, Hades, provided the inspiration for our legends of Hell.

The Irin – The Irin are a benevolent race of winged aliens from the parallel dimension of Basilea. They have been assigned to patrol the shadow realm on the edge of our dimension to protect the Human Race from an Archon invasion.

Eliel (An *Irin* warrior) – With wings concealed, Eliel appears to be an attractive 21 year-old woman, but she's visited our world for thousands of years and walked the streets of ancient Babylon and Rome.

Kareina (An *Archon* Commander) – Kareina was sent to the Earth-realm to prepare the way for the Archon invasion. Now she is plotting the final destruction of the Human Race.

PROLOGUE

Wormwood

IN ORBIT AROUND THE PLANET JUPITER

It was a big, ugly rock, as comets usually are — a "dirty snowball" nearly a mile across — billions of tons of stone and rock-hard ice spinning silently in the darkness of space.

The rock had suffered many collisions over the centuries. Its face was now pockmarked with gashes and craters.

One section of the rock had come close to being ripped away entirely. A large chunk of rock, a thousand feet in diameter, was now anchored to the rest of the comet by a slender neck less than fifty feet across, giving the rock the appearance of a lopsided dumbbell.

The rock had originally been part of the Kuiper belt, a vast cloud of rocks and planetoids, circling the sun beyond the orbit of Neptune.

For countless eons, it had maintained a steady orbit. On planet Earth, the dinosaurs had come and gone. For thousands of years, an ice age gripped Earth's continents, then the glaciers finally receded. The Great Wars were fought, and human civilization slowly re-emerged. The pyramids were built.

The Roman Empire rose and fell. Still, the big, ugly rock continued its lonely trek.

The year Columbus discovered America, the ugly rock suffered a glancing blow from a smaller rock that slightly altered its orbit, nudging it closer to the sun and putting it on a trajectory that would eventually intersect the orbit of Neptune.

In 1912, a few weeks after the passenger ship RMS Titanic struck an iceberg and sank, the ugly rock encountered the planet Neptune, bringing another shift in its orbit. The ugly rock did not strike Neptune. Instead, the gravity of Neptune ripped the rock from its peaceful orbit and flung it toward the inner solar system, headed almost directly into the sun.

As the ugly rock approached the inner solar system, the sun's heat began to warm the ice that made up much of its surface. The ice began to sublimate, evaporating into the vacuum of space. As it did so, a trail of vapor began streaming from the rock's surface. A transformation was beginning. The ugly rock was about to become a beautiful comet.

But as the rock passed the orbit of Jupiter, its path was again interrupted. The massive gravity of the solar system's largest planet captured the rock and pulled it in.

Caught in Jupiter's gravity, it looked at first as though the ugly rock might collide with Jupiter, but as it approached the planet, its momentum increased, allowing it to swing around Jupiter and be flung back out into space.

As the rock attempted to pull away from Jupiter, however, the giant planet's gravity held it fast, stealing its momentum. Lacking the energy to escape from Jupiter's grasp, the rock swung around Jupiter in a long, slow arc, until it was pulled back in to approach the planet again.

Over and over again this process repeated. Though the comet's new orbit was eccentric and unstable, it was not eccentric enough to cause it to impact Jupiter, nor was it unstable enough to escape. If nothing else had happened to perturb its orbit, the comet might have continued to orbit the planet Jupiter until the end of time.

PART ONE: ROGER

Chapter One: Dragonfire

THE GREAT PORTAL OF ABADON, HADES

Roger was back. It seemed impossible. In fact, it *was* impossible.

Roger was dead.

Lys vividly recalled the moment of her brother's death. It was indelibly seared in her memory.

Lys had gone into Hades, along with Roger and Michael, in an attempt to rescue Jamie Thatcher from the Archons. Against all odds, they'd succeeded.

But as they were leaving the city of Abadon, they found their path blocked by three Archon guards. Praetor Hewett, the repulsive, corpulent, toad-like human who'd served as their guide, had betrayed them. To enhance his own position in Hades, he'd consigned the four friends to a life of slavery and torture and the entire Earth-realm to terrible devastation.

"In exchange for betraying you," Hewett boasted to Lys, wattles jiggling. "I'm getting spacious new living quarters — big enough to enlarge my harem! There'll be a special room there just for you,

Miss Johnston, and you'll never be lonely. I'm planning to spend a great deal of time with you. After all, I paid fifty shekels of silver for you!"

"You bastard!" Lys screamed in rage, driving the hardest punch she could into his immense gut. Then, seeing that his stomach was too well padded for her fist to produce an effect, she brought her knee up forcefully into his groin.

Startled and hurt, the toad staggered back a step and dropped his sword.

The three Archon guards were moving in quickly to take control of the situation, but Roger Johnston was faster.

Taking up Hewett's fallen sword, Roger activated the Irin life-force that had been given him by Mendrion for just such an emergency. His body began to glow with a brilliant, white light. He felt a life and energy he'd never imagined possible flowing through every part of his being.

Roger hadn't handled a sword since a fencing course his second year in collage but the Irin life-force more than compensated for his inexperience. Shifting the blade in his hand, he willed the life-force energy to flow through his hand and out to the end of the sword. The blade began to glow with a dazzling, white light.

The toad instinctively reached out to Roger to retrieve his sword, but with his unexpected new strength, Roger dispatched him with one flick of his wrist. The glowing sword slashed deeply into the toad's abdomen, which erupted in greasy flames. Praetor Hewett stood for a moment, mouth open, uncomprehending, then fell over backward, dead.

But Roger had already turned his attention to the perplexed Archons. The Archon guards had killed many humans, both in Hades and the Earth-realm, but they'd never seen a human with the life-energy of an Irin. They held back for a moment, hesitant to approach him.

High overhead, a dragon had also noticed the display of Irin energy, and was diving in their direction.

Seeing the dragon, Roger shouted, "Lys, get to the stone circle and open that portal NOW. You must get Michael and Jamie out of here!"

"Not without you!"

"There's no time to argue!" he shouted as the three Archons moved to surround him. "Get that damn portal open now or we'll all be dead! I know what I'm doing."

The Archon guards were far more experienced with a sword, but Roger had the advantage of the Irin life-force. One touch of his glowing blade would bring instant death.

Roger slashed at one of the Archons, who quickly backed away. Then, as another Archon moved close behind him, he swung around and drove his glowing blade home. The Archon exploded in flames.

The two remaining Archons moved more carefully now, but continued to press the fight. The dragon was getting closer.

"Lys, *GO!*" Roger screamed again. "We're out of time!"

Lys hesitated another moment, but knew Roger was right. She and Michael half carried Jamie into the circle of standing stones, where Jamie collapsed unconscious. Casey, the terrified teenage girl they'd invited to join them in their escape attempt, followed a few steps behind.

Lys took a deep breath and prepared to open the portal.

Standing in the center of the great slabs of rock, the now-familiar flow of unlearned words poured from deep within her, rising to a crescendo that reverberated between the dimensions. The overcast sky parted, and light beamed into the darkness, illuminating the four.

But Lys's eyes were still fixed on Roger. So far, he was holding his own, but the Irin life-force was beginning to fade.

With tears in her eyes, Lys cried, "Roger, come *now*, it's not too late! You can make it!"

Roger glanced at the circle of stones and noticed the portal had begun to open. It was just 200 feet away, two-thirds the length of a football field. If he ran, he might just make it, but it was taking all of his effort to keep the Archons at bay, and the dragon was almost upon him.

He thought of Lys, who might be enslaved in Hades for the rest of her life if she did not escape within the next few minutes. He thought of Jamie, whom he now realized had always been the love of his life. He thought of Casey, her innocence stolen, barbarically tortured in the arena at an age when she should have been texting with friends and cheering at high school football games. Finally, he thought of the Archon threat to the entire Earth-realm, of the arena being duplicated thousands of times over on every continent. *Hell on earth!* Roger knew what was at stake, and his choice was clear.

The dragon had paid little notice when the portal opened. The opening of a portal was a regular event here. It had not even noticed the others standing illuminated in the center of the stone circle. The dragon was fully focused on him. As long as the Irin life-force remained, it appeared to the dragon that one of the hated Irin was doing battle with Archon guards in the very heart of Hades. That held the dragon's attention. If Roger were to try to join the others, the dragon's attention would shift, imperiling them all.

"I can't go with you, Sis," Roger shouted. "Tell Jamie I love her... I've always loved her!"

The Irin life-force was nearly depleted, but Roger remained the focus of the dragon's attack. As the four felt themselves drawn into the now-open portal, the shadow of the dragon fell across Roger. A bellowing roar split the air; then a torrent of dragonfire spewed from the beast's mouth, instantly vaporizing both Roger and the Archon guards.

And so Roger Johnston had died — incinerated in a blast of dragonfire.

There was no way he could have survived the dragon's attack, and even if he had, he would have been stranded in Hades once the portal closed.

But Roger was back.
He showed up at the door one night, smiling.

Chapter Two: Roger's Return

IONA HOUSE – THE ISLAND OF IONA, SCOTLAND

They all remembered the night Roger returned.

The Iona synaxis had just moved into the recently completed Iona House. It was a time of heady excitement.

The week they moved in, Patrick and Lys announced their engagement, which came as a surprise to no one. They'd decided to hold their wedding on Iona. Erin Fletcher volunteered to fly both sets of parents to Scotland on her private jet for the ceremony in late August.

Casey, the teenage girl they'd rescued from Hades, had joined the synaxis and was thriving. Catherine Campbell had taken Casey under her wing and was teaching her to hunt, as well as instructing her in the culinary arts.

To show off her new skills, Casey had fixed Catherine's 'world-famous' spicy venison stew and invited the entire synaxis to a feast. They had all eaten 'till they could eat no more, then retreated to the living area and spent an hour in relaxed conversation, sipping their favorite wines.

As they talked, Erin shared the latest email from Holmes and Piper, reporting on the progress of the synaxis groups. The growth-rate was staggering. From about 90 groups earlier in the summer, the current estimate was close to 300.

The multiplication was already producing measurable results. As humans were empowered to use their gifts, the Archons were being driven back and their schemes frustrated. Crime rates in many areas had dropped. There were more and more instances of incurable illnesses being healed. With the aid of the synaxis members who had the "second sight" gift, a number of terrorist attacks had been thwarted.

Responding to the encouraging email, Patrick suggested they celebrate by opening a few more bottles of wine, an idea that won hearty approval from the entire group.

Everyone seemed to be enjoying the evening except Jamie Thatcher. Jamie sat in silence, feeling like an intruder at someone else's party.

She felt her life was in ruins. A few weeks earlier she'd lost her sister, Becky, her only remaining family—vaporized in a nuclear fireball unleashed by her boss Carrington. Then in rapid succession she'd lost her job, her home, and what she'd thought was her future. The only positive event in the last few weeks had been the restoration of her relationship with Roger Johnston.

Jamie had dated Roger her last two years of college. It had been the happiest time of her life.

She'd always assumed they'd get married, but as graduation approached, Jamie got her acceptance letter from the Computer Science Graduate Program at Stanford, located in California's Silicon Valley. Jamie's specialty was computer science, and Stanford was the top-ranked computer science school in the world. It seemed a no-brainer.

Meanwhile, Roger was accepted by Yale Medical School in Connecticut, an opportunity he knew he could not pass up. They'd talked for hours, trying to find a way to keep their relationship going, but could see no way to make it work.

They'd gone their separate ways and within a few years had completely lost contact with each other.

But earlier this year, an incredible set of circumstances had brought Roger back into Jamie's life. Something within them both reawakened. Surprisingly, their relationship seemed to pick up where it had left off many years earlier.

But then, Jamie was kidnapped by Archon warriors and taken to the parallel dimension of Hades where she was savagely tortured. Against the advice of the Irin, Roger led a rescue team that succeeded in saving her, but was himself killed in the process.

After years of separation, Jamie had hoped she and Roger would finally have a life together, but his death crushed all of her hopes. She'd spent the last few weeks in mourning... for Roger, for herself, and for the dreams she'd once held.

As Jamie sat in the midst of the joyful celebration contemplating the bleakness of her future, there was a knock on the door.

"I'll get it," Jamie said, thankful for an excuse to distance herself from the happy gathering.

Jamie walked to the door, turned the knob and gave a gentle tug.

As the door swung open, Jamie's eyes widened. For a full minute she stood frozen, unmoving, in total silence. Jamie couldn't comprehend what she was seeing, and had no idea how to respond. Tears began welling in her eyes. Her mouth struggled to speak one word—a hoarse whisper, barely audible... *"Roger?"*

The man standing in the doorway smiled warmly, "Hi, Thatcher."

After an eternity of silence, she finally found words, "Are you *real?*"

"I assure you, I am real."

"But Lys said you were *dead*. She said a dragon had incinerated you."

Roger paused a moment, then said. "I *was* dead... but now I'm alive. But I assure you that I'm not a ghost. I'm fully human." He extended his right hand to her.

Still not believing her eyes, Jamie tentatively reached out and touched Roger's hand.

Buoyed by the reality of his touch, Jamie could no longer restrain herself. In a sudden rush of emotion, she threw herself, sobbing, into Roger's arms.

The rest of the synaxis by this time had taken notice of what was happening at the door. They crowded around Roger and Jamie, awestruck and confused.

They'd all talked late into the night.

Roger explained that when the surge of

dragonfire engulfed him, there had been no pain. Instead, he found himself instantly transported to Hi-Ouranos, the highest of all realms, to stand in the presence of the High King.

The High King told him that because he had freely sacrificed his life to save those he loved, Hades could not hold him. The High King himself had rescued Roger.

Bombarded with questions about his time away, Roger revealed very little. He said that there was much he was not permitted to say. Only that great changes were coming for the world, and that he had been sent back for a purpose.

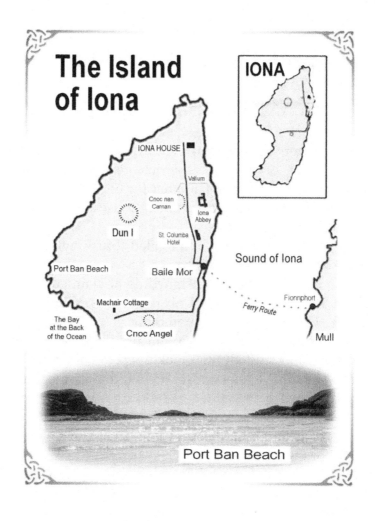

Port Ban Beach

Chapter Three: Walking Iona

ISLAND OF IONA, SCOTLAND

Roger Johnston extracted the cork with a slight pop. After pouring a generous glass of Cabernet Sauvignon for Jamie and another for himself, he made his way to the rear deck of Iona House where Jamie was already relaxing.

Jamie looked up and smiled, brushing a wisp of ebony hair from her eyes.

"Hi, Thatcher," he smiled as he handed her a glass. "This is that new Cabernet I was telling you about. Let me know what you think."

Jamie swirled the wine in the glass, held it to her nose and sniffed, then took a sip. "This is really nice," she said. "A lot of cabs are too dry for me, but I like this one."

Roger took a seat next to her.

This had been their evening ritual almost every night for the past week.

They sat for a while in silence, sipping their wine and enjoying a beautiful mid-summer evening on Iona.

To the west, the sky was still glowing with the last light of day, while the first faint stars glimmered over the eastern horizon.

The Sound of Iona lay quiet in the cool night air. The lights of the little village of Fionnphort shimmered and danced across the water. To the north, a small fishing boat was plowing a watery furrow, as a weary fisherman hurried home to a hot meal and a cold pint.

Further to the east, Mull's red granite mountains had already faded to near black in the dying light.

Jamie leaned back in her chair, experiencing a sense of peace and contentment she hadn't thought possible.

A Jewish friend had once told Jamie about a Hebrew word that has no real equivalent in English. It was the word *shalom*. Her friend said it referred to a state of absolute perfection, encompassing complete peace, provision, health, and well-being.

Shalom. That's what I'm feeling this evening. Perfect contentment.

Part of her *shalom* came from living on Iona. Since the opening of the Iona portal, the Island of Iona had become an Irin stronghold.

The Irin, a benevolent race from the parallel world of Basilea, now interacted freely with humans on Iona, and the atmosphere of the island had been transformed. Stepping off the ferry to Iona now was like stepping into another world. The sense of well-being was so tangible; first-time visitors were sometimes moved to tears as they encountered the power of the place.

Because of the Irin presence on the island, the malevolent beings known as Archons could no longer approach. The result was a place virtually without evil. There was no crime on the island. No screaming, angry voices were heard. No one lived in fear.

But the contentment Jamie was feeling tonight went far beyond anything related to Iona.

Most of her feeling of *shalom* tonight was a direct result of her relationship with Roger.

Jamie had been surprised at how quickly life with Roger had settled into a normal rhythm, breakfasting together in the mornings, seeing each other from time to time during the day, and on pleasant evenings, sharing a glass of wine on the deck at sunset.

Erin had recently assigned Jamie to work on a new project—putting together a secure computer network to enable instant communication between every synaxis on earth. It wasn't a difficult assignment for her; and it felt good to be doing something useful.

But the project left her with plenty of free time, and she and Roger had taken full advantage of it.

Yesterday afternoon, they had decided to explore the southern end of the island. Neither Jamie or Roger had been on Iona long, though Jamie had been there a few weeks longer than Roger, so whenever they had a chance, they would put on their hiking boots, pick up a map, and go exploring.

Jamie and Roger always enjoyed their walks together, but yesterday's walk was different, and it ended in a way Jamie had not anticipated.

Jamie had spent the morning testing the new synaxis network and working out a few of the remaining bugs. She was ready for a break.

They left Iona House just after lunch, stopping

by the Spar shop to pick up some cheese, fruit, and other goodies for a relaxed picnic, along with a bottle of their favorite wine.

They'd never been to the southern end of the island, but since Iona had just gone a week without rain, they hoped the normally-boggy paths would be more passable than usual.

Their outing began with a leisurely stroll southward along the eastern shore. It was a clear summer day, pleasantly warm, but with a stiff wind blowing from the north bringing gusts that whipped their hair around as they walked.

"This reminds me of the walks we used to take back in Colorado." Roger said.

"I was just thinking about that," Jamie smiled. "I loved those times. We'd head out from campus, walk all the way to Scott Carpenter Park, and spend the whole afternoon talking, reading, and sharing our dreams."

"Those of us without photographic memories actually had to spend *some* of that time studying." Roger chided.

"But I loved those walks to the park," he continued. "Colorado was so beautiful. I can still see the majestic front range of the Rockies towering over the city of Boulder."

"Colorado was beautiful," Jamie said, "but I'll still take Iona."

Glancing around as he walked, Roger couldn't help but agree. The sea between Iona and Mull seemed to flow like a river, driven by the strong north wind. The water quivered. The wind and sun created a tapestry of shimmering hues.

The island itself was extraordinary in its stark beauty. Multicolored wildflowers were splattered everywhere. Twittering birds fluttered around them while two, majestic, white-tailed sea eagles soared effortlessly above the coast. Creation on Iona seemed wild and unbridled, untouched by civilization. Jamie and Roger felt like they'd come to the end of the world.

Their first stop was St Columba Bay, also known as Coracle Bay. Located at the southernmost tip of the island, it was the place where Saint Columba and his 12 disciples had first landed on the island in his skin-covered boat back in A.D. 563.

The beach at Coracle Bay was a pebble beach, and the pebbles reflected the extraordinary geological makeup of the island, with quartz, granite, flint, mica, marble and more. Among the dazzling array of pinks, reds, blacks, and whites, were slivers of translucent, green serpentine, "Iona Jewels," which had been polished by the wave action of the sea.

Roger and Jamie stayed a long time in the rocky little cove, talking and laughing about their past, while skimming flat stones across the waves.

Jamie reached down and picked up a particularly large flat stone and tossed it like a Frisbee with all her might. It slid from her hand and flashed across the water, skipping at least seven times before it finally sank.

"Wow. That's the champion of the day!" Roger laughed.

He tried to outdo her with an even larger stone,

but it sank after the second skip.

Leaving Columba's bay, they hiked the sheep trails, traversing the moorlands to the western side of the island. At its end, their trail led down a narrow valley to a broad, crescent-shaped, white-sand beach—a place called The Bay at the Back of the Ocean.

The Bay at the Back of the Ocean is one of the most famous spots on Iona. It looks like a beach from a Caribbean travel brochure that somehow had been transported to a rocky Scottish isle. It only lacked a few palm trees to complete the tropical illusion.

Roger and Jamie walked quietly along the shore, squinting their eyes against the windblown sand. Oystercatchers and starlings pattered on the tideline. The fierce north wind raised whitecaps on the slate-grey sea. They both laughed as they watched two seals playing in the surf.

Jamie pointed to a small bed and breakfast perched on the embankment overlooking the beach. "Lys and Catherine used to live right up there at Machair Cottage before Iona House was finished.

Noting the big picture windows on the second floor, Roger commented, "I'll bet the sunsets over the Atlantic were spectacular. I can see how Lys would have enjoyed living there."

Jamie was silent for a moment, then said, "I'm so glad Lys is here with us on Iona. I remember when we were dating, she flew up from Texas several times to see you. She was just a kid then, but I really liked her."

"My little sister has become an incredibly strong woman," Roger said. "We would never have come this far without her. I'm so glad things have worked out between her and Patrick."

Passing the Bay at the Back of the Ocean, they continued north to what had become their favorite place on the island, a secluded little beach known as *Port Ban.*

Port Ban has a reputation as the most beautiful beach in all of the Western Isles. Surrounded by rugged outcrops of rock to the north and south, the beach is sheltered from the wind and is known for its pristine, white sand and shallow water.

Finally out of the wind, Roger and Jamie strolled peacefully to the center of the beach, listening to the rolling waves and enjoying the warm sand crunching under their feet.

After taking off their hiking boots, Jamie spread out a blanket. Roger poured the wine, and they both enjoyed a relaxed picnic together, as the sun moved lower in the sky.

Running her hand through the soft warm sand and smelling the fresh ocean scent made the day seem surreal. A warm sensation ran through Jamie's body bringing tears to her eyes.

It was then that she'd first remembered her friend's untranslatable word, *Shalom! Perfect peace. Perfect contentment. Total well-being. That's what this feels like.*

Roger and Jamie talked for hours, but neither was aware of time passing. As they conversed, their surroundings faded into the background: The sounds of seagulls cawing and screeching... flapping wings... waves crashing against the sandy shore. They were oblivious to it all.

Finally Roger grew quiet, "Jamie, I can't believe we're together again. So many times I thought we'd blown it.

"I've thought a lot about our times back in Colorado when we picnicked in the park and shared our dreams. I knew even then that you would always be the love of my life.

"But for years, I thought all those hopes and dreams were lost. I saw no way they could be recovered.

"But now we're here together, on this beach at the end of the world. Somehow we've been given another chance."

As the sun was about to set, they both stood to their feet. Jamie started to roll up their blanket, but it was clear Roger was not yet ready to leave.

"Let's walk down to the tide line. There's something I want to show you."

Jamie glanced across the beach. She saw seaweed, shells, and a few pieces of driftwood, but nothing out of the ordinary.

She slipped her hand into Roger's and they strolled to the tide line, then stood together side-by-side watching the sun complete its daily trek.

As the sun was about to touch the horizon, Roger slid an object from his pocket, taking care to keep it concealed in his hand. It was something he had purchased in Oban two days earlier.

"What's that, Roger?"

"It's something I should have given you a long, long time ago."

Dropping to one knee, he held out a tiny black box and flipped open the lid.

Tears welled in Jamie's eyes as she saw its contents glistening in the light of the setting sun.

"It's time, Jamie… It's time for *everything* we've lost to be restored."

Jamie felt overwhelmed—she was unable to speak. Tears were rolling down her cheeks.

Roger paused a moment, then continued, "In case you haven't guessed it, Jamie, I'm asking you to marry me."

As Jamie accepted his proposal, she had no way of knowing that they were both about to enter a battle that would determine the fate of every human being on earth.

PART TWO: THE SHEIKH

Chapter Three:
Marissa's Story

THE DESERT OF NORTHERN IRAQ

Her head was pounding, her brain about to explode, and her stomach in deep distress. She sensed she could puke at any moment.

This is one hell of a hangover... Marissa mumbled as she fought her way back to consciousness. *It feels like I've been run over by a whole fleet of eighteen wheelers. Every part of my body aches!* She tried to remember the night before, but could not.

She opened her eyes to look around, but could see only darkness. She was totally disoriented. *Where am I?*

Attempting to relieve an ache in the small of her back, Marissa tried to turn over, but her body was stiff and her movement somehow constrained. Trying again, she discovered, to her horror, that her wrists and ankles were bound in chains.

Marissa made one more effort to roll over, determined to relieve the grinding pain in her back, but found there was nowhere to roll. Solid walls enclosed her on both sides. With the limited mobility her chains allowed, she reached out to examine the space of her confinement.

What she found terrified her. She was enclosed in a wooden box barely larger than she was. Her elbows scraped the box's rough plank sides when she tried to move her arms, and the lid hovered mere inches above her face. She pushed upward against the lid with all of her strength, but it was securely fastened.

Rising panic engulfed her. *I'm in a coffin! ...Have I been buried alive?*

But no... she could feel the continuing rumble of a powerful diesel engine and the movement of a large vehicle traversing badly potholed roads. She was locked in a box, but she was being taken somewhere.

What's happened to me? How did I get here? Marissa shook her head to clear the cobwebs.

Flickers of memory began to come... disjointed images of angry men brandishing automatic weapons, women weeping, children screaming...

Finally the repressed horror of the last four days flooded her consciousness.

Dr. Marissa Kobani had grown up in small Iraqi Christian village a hundred miles north of Baghdad, but her family had immigrated to the US when she was a teenager. Always a quick learner, she'd excelled in school, graduating from high school a year early and finishing near the top of her class in college. She was accepted to a prestigious medical school where she also graduated with honors.

An ill-advised marriage her second year in

college had fallen prey to the intense pressures of medical school. As her academic schedule demanded more and more of her time, her husband became resentful, then abusive. The marriage ended in divorce shortly before her graduation. At the end of her residency, she found herself with an MD, but very little direction for her future.

That was when she began hearing the horror stories from her home country. With the rise of ISIS, the so-called Islamic State, tens of thousands of civilians had been brutally slaughtered in northern Iraq and Syria. Whole villages of Iraqi Christians and Yazidis were obliterated — the men butchered and the women enslaved. The result was a humanitarian crisis, as thousands of terrorized Iraqis and Syrians fled their homes in one of the largest and swiftest mass movements of people in history. Huge refugee camps sprang up just beyond the areas of ISIS control.

Responding to this crisis in her homeland, Marissa signed up to serve on a medical relief team with the World Health Organization. With her fluency in both Arabic and English coupled with her medical training, she was soon leading her own emergency response team.

Headquartered in an overcrowded refugee camp 350 miles north of Baghdad, she also operated mobile clinics in the surrounding villages one day a week.

The work was demanding and exhausting, but she found her time in Iraq to be one of the most meaningful experiences of her life. From distributing blankets and hygiene kits, setting broken bones, operating prenatal care clinics, and treating various infections with life-saving antibiotics, she began to see hopelessness replaced by hope.

Four days ago, she'd taken a team to Erba Abdol, a village of about 600 Kurdish-speaking Yazidis located sixty miles northwest of her camp. Her good friend, Hashim Kamil went along as a medical assistant. Also with them was a local Kurdish-speaking interpreter named Azad Hariri.

Erba Abdol was an isolated village sitting at the base of Mount Abdol, a massif of dun-colored rock set on a bleak, dusty plain.

Stopping atop a rise just outside the town, Marissa got out of the van and scanned the village, letting her luxuriant raven hair rustle softly in the breeze.

By any measure, Marissa was a beautiful woman, with flawless olive skin, wide-set dark brown eyes, and full lips. As a Christian Iraqi, she didn't feel constrained to conceal her hair as Islamic women did, but allowed it to flow freely, casually tossing it to the side when she knelt to examine patients.

The village on the plain before her was not a pretty place. She'd been there several times. The town square was an expanse of hard-packed dirt, with little vegetation. Packs of emaciated dogs rummaged through garbage piled beside the crumbling walls of the houses. The stench of burning trash assaulted the nostrils.

Scanning the horizon carefully, Marissa detected no sign of danger. She took a deep breath and let it out slowly. This was not the kind of place she would have chosen to spend a day, but it was a place she was desperately needed. And she only made the trip to Erba Abdol once a month.

Following her normal procedure, she and Hashim set up the mobile clinic on the north end of the town square, pitching a canopy by the side of the van and setting out a table, two chairs, and a folding cot. The line of patients formed immediately. She had spent two hours examining patients and tending wounds when she was distracted by a disturbance at the western edge of the village. There were sounds of sporadic gunfire and the tumult of people running and screaming, with one word echoing above the din: *"ISIS!"*

Peering down the street, Marissa saw a large convoy of ISIS vehicles approaching from the west.

A sense of terror gripped Marissa as she frantically tried to think through her options. The Islamists were mere minutes away. There was no time to escape and nowhere to hide. She was in serious trouble.

The Islamic State had a reputation for barbarity unparalleled in modern times. They had repeatedly shocked the world with televised beheadings, crucifixions, and the burning alive of a captured Jordanian pilot. Perhaps most distressing was their institution of sexual slavery. ISIS taught that non-Muslim women, such as those from the Christian and Yazidi minorities, were *kafirah*, or infidels, fit only to be enslaved or killed. Some estimate that since the rise of ISIS, as many as 30,000 *kafirah* women had been taken captive. The few women fortunate enough to escape their ISIS captivity brought back horror stories of being stripped naked and sold like cattle in the slave markets of Mosul and Raqqa, to be repeatedly raped and tortured by their captors.

Before Marissa headed out from the refugee camp that morning, she'd checked the reports of ISIS activity, but nothing had been reported within a hundred miles of her location. Yet the fleet of road-worn vehicles flying black and white ISIS banners that even now were disgorging their fighters at the edge of the village provided ample evidence that the reports were wrong. The barbarians were at the gate.

The next few hours were a nightmare. ISIS warriors brandishing automatic weapons went from house-to-house through the village and forced every resident into the main square. They demanded valuables and the villagers dutifully retrieved their most coveted possessions, dropping rings, jewelry and fistfuls of money onto a blanket spread on the ground in the middle of the square.

When all the villagers had assembled in the square, the ISIS commander pointed to a jeweled dagger protruding from the village leader's belt. It was a family heirloom, the man's most treasured possession. The man placed his hand on the dagger's hilt and firmly shook his head no. Without hesitation, the ISIS leader raised his gun and pumped a bullet into the old man's head, then walked over and ripped the dagger from his belt.

Any hopes that the barbarians would be content with looting valuables was soon dashed.

The men and boys of the village were

separated from the women and marched down a side street to the fields beyond. Despite their protests, Marissa's friend Hashim and their interpreter were forced to join them. The chatter of automatic weapons a few moments later left little doubt as to their fate.

The ISIS warriors then lined up the women. The older women and those not deemed "attractive" were told to take the babies and younger children and stand at the far side of the square. The remaining women and girls—the ones who had passed ISIS screening—were taken at gunpoint down another street to a line of open-bed trucks. Those who resisted were shot. As the terrified women were loaded into the trucks, sounds of gunfire from the village square confirmed the doom of those they had left behind.

Crowded into a truck with more than thirty other women, Marissa felt numb. The barbarians had just murdered her friends in cold blood, along with more than half the population of the village. She'd read the UN reports of ISIS raids, but had always assumed they were exaggerated. Yet what just happened in Erba Abdol was exactly what those reports had described.

Given no food or water, the women were driven for five hours to a larger town where they were ushered into a warehouse. The place had been prepared to receive them. There were mattresses, plates and utensils, and food and water for hundreds of people. *This was all planned in advance!*

The women were confined in the warehouse for four days, fed one meal a day and given water occasionally. There were no bathing facilities, and a row of buckets along the far wall served as the only restroom.

Life in the warehouse was horrific beyond description. Close to a hundred and fifty women and girls had been thrust into the sparse room — all of them struggling to process the fact that their fathers and mothers, husbands and brothers, sons and baby daughters had just been brutally murdered. With no way to cope with such overwhelming grief, the room echoed continually with the sounds of weeping, wracking sobs, and loud wailing. Most of the women had not yet even dared to ponder their own fate.

On the third day Marissa noticed a woman and girl sitting along the wall, clinging to each other and weeping. As Marissa walked over and sat beside them, the woman looked up, tears still flowing down her cheeks. The woman was about thirty years old and pretty, with reddish blonde hair and pale blue eyes, something not uncommon among Yazidis. The girl, who Marissa guessed to be about twelve, had blue eyes also.

Hungry for someone to talk to, Marissa asked, "Do you speak English?"

The woman sadly shook her head.

"Do you speak any Arabic?"

"A little," the woman replied.

The woman seemed willing to talk, though her limited knowledge of Arabic made communication difficult.

Marissa found that the woman's name was Jinan, and the girl was Besma. They were not mother and daughter. They'd been neighbors. But standing together in the village square, both Jinan and Besma had lost their families in one horrific hour. Jinan's husband and son, along with Besma's father and brothers, had been marched out of town and shot. Jinan's daughter Narin had been only three years old, too young to make the ISIS cull, while Besma's mother had been in her 40's and deemed "not attractive." Both had also met their fate at the hands of ISIS. Now Jinan and Besma had only each other.

Listening to their story, Marissa could not hold back her tears. She wondered how many other Iraqi women could now share similar stories.

At last, the women were taken from the warehouse and loaded onto a fleet of busses. Curtains at the windows of their bus prevented Marissa from identifying any landmarks, but the bus drove for six hours straight. It was late afternoon when they were escorted off the bus and marched at gunpoint to a multi-story building that had once been a children's school.

A hand-painted sign over the door now identified the building as the *sabaya* market, the slave market. Busses from other locations were also unloading human cargo. This was auction day and crowds of warriors in ISIS garb were waiting outside the place, eyeing the women as they were herded into the building.

The first stop was a crowded admitting room, where bearded men sitting behind a long table asked the women questions and took a photograph of each one.

Identifying a man who seemed to be in charge,

Marissa saw her chance to appeal for help. "Excuse me, sir," She said, smiling her most professional smile, "I am a doctor. I'm here in Iraq with the World Health Organization. I need to contact my superiors. If you could please let me use a phone..."

"Silence!" The man exploded in rage, spraying her face with spittle. He glared at her menacingly. "You are *not* a doctor! You are *kafirah*..." he screamed, slapping her hard across the face.

"You are an infidel woman and a captured slave of the *mujahedeen!*" He repeated it again for emphasis. "You are a female slave... nothing more! From now on you will do only what the *mujahedeen* tell you. Now go to your room and wait!"

Escorted from the admitting room, the women were placed in former classrooms, jammed forty or fifty to a room until it was their turn to be sold.

The classroom was oppressively hot, with little air circulation. Marissa glanced around at the other women. The oldest was probably in her late-thirties but there were also girls as young as nine. The women were all in shock. Marissa sensed that many of them still had not grasped what was about to happen to them.

Around midnight, a man came to the door of their room to announce that their turn had come. The women were led to the auction hall in groups of five.

The auction hall appeared to have once been a school cafeteria, or assembly area. Paint was peeling from the dingy walls and the bare concrete floor was stained with urine and blood. Across one end of the room a rough wooden platform had been erected, two feet high, twenty-four feet long, and eight feet wide. Rows of old wooden and plastic chairs filled the rest of the room. Even at this late hour, more than half of the chairs were occupied. The atmosphere was a haze of cigarette smoke and hashish.

Hearing a babel of voices, Marissa noted that a good number of the assembled fighters were foreigners. In addition to Iraqis and Syrians she picked out the voices of Iranians, Afghanis, and a number of Russian-speaking *mujahedeen* from Chechnya. There were even a few English speakers. They were all ISIS warriors—brutal, coldblooded killers who had come to the market tonight to purchase an attractive young woman to rape and abuse. The thought made Marissa want to vomit.

Entering the auction hall, the five women in Marissa's group were directed to ascend the stage. At the far end of the stage stood the auctioneer, a whip in one hand and the hilt of a silver dagger protruding from the belt of his robe. Extending his whip toward the traumatized women, he announced loudly, "By the will of Allah, we have lawfully raided and captured these *kafirah* females and driven them like sheep, by the edge of the sword. Now we may do to them as we please!"

One by one, he came to the women, announced their name, age, and home village, then ordered them to disrobe, enforcing his command with painful lashes from his whip until they obeyed. Marissa watched in horror as each one was forced to remove their clothing and stand cringing in shame, before the leering crowd. Marissa was the last woman in line.

When one of the women refused to disrobe, despite repeated lashes, two burly guards mounted the stage and literally ripped the clothing from her body. Forced into compliance, the terrified woman stood weeping before the crowd, futilely attempting to conceal her nakedness with her hands.

Of course, the barbarian audience considered all of this to be great entertainment. They responded to the spectacle with hoots, hollers, and raucous cheers, their excitement growing by the minute as they waited for the bidding to begin.

Finally the auctioneer came to Marissa. She looked him in the eye without flinching. *They will do to me what they're going to do, but I will NOT give them the satisfaction of showing fear! I will not cower before them!*

When he gave the order to disrobe, she slipped out of her shirt without hesitation, dropped her pants, removed her undergarments, and stood before the startled barbarians, calmly and defiantly naked. Her unexpected brazenness caused a gasp to go up from the crowd.

The auctioneer stood in silence for a moment, mouth open, not sure how to respond.

Then he noticed a small gold cross dangling between Marissa's breasts, a gift from her mother when she'd first moved to America.

At the sight of the cross, the man was enraged. "Infidel *pig!*" He hissed, savagely tearing it from her neck. He gazed at the hated symbol of Christianity for a moment, then spat on it, threw it to the floor, and stomped it with his heel.

Marissa calmly stood her ground, glaring at him, showing no emotion but utter contempt.

Again the auctioneer was dumbfounded. An infidel woman was standing naked on his auction block, showing no trace of fear, and to make matters worse she was treating him with open disdain. The audience had fallen silent, the warriors shifting uncomfortably in their chairs. He was losing face. The auction was not going well at all.

Attempting to recoup the situation, the auctioneer exploded with rage, "You are an infidel *whore!*" He hissed. "For that you will die!"

Grabbing Marissa's long, flowing hair with his left hand, he jerked her head back as he slipped the dagger from his belt and raised its razor-sharp blade to her throat, determined to make her pay the ultimate price for her impudence.

Chapter Four:
The Sheikh's Palace

THE DESERT OF EASTERN JORDAN

As the auctioneer was about to slit Marissa's throat, a deep voice thundered across the room. "Stop!"

The crowd parted as a large man in the garb of an ISIS high commander made his way across the room to stand before Marissa.

Glaring at the auctioneer, he said firmly, "Release her! Now!"

The startled auctioneer hesitated a moment, then grudgingly complied. "Yes, Abdullah."

The auctioneer released his grip on Marissa's hair and took a step back, still clenching the dagger tightly in his right hand.

The high commander looked Marissa over carefully, then laughed, "This infidel woman is not only attractive. She has *spirit!*

"I'm meeting with the sheikh tomorrow and must take him a gift. As all *mujahedeen* know, the sheikh has a great appreciation for high-spirited female slaves, especially ones as lovely as this!" Fixing his eyes on the auctioneer, he declared, "I'm taking this *kafirah* as my gift for the sheikh!"

Without waiting for a response from the auctioneer, he turned to Marissa. "Put your clothing on and follow me. I'll give you proper garments and something to eat before the journey. We leave in two hours."

That was it. For Marissa, the auction was over.

As Marissa pulled on her clothes and followed the man from the room, she looked at the ISIS high commander with confusion. Was this man her rescuer? She detected no kindness in his voice, but at least she was out of the slave market.

Perhaps her nightmare was almost over. If she could explain to this mysterious sheikh who she was, he might agree to release her in exchange for a ransom.

Sitting in what had once been the office of the school's principal, the man the auctioneer called *Abdullah* gave Marissa a sparse meal of stale bread and canned fish, washed down with a glass of overly-sweetened tea. When she'd finished eating, he ordered her to remove her infidel clothing and gave her a black burka that covered her body from head to toe, leaving only a small mesh window before her eyes. He then bound her hands and feet in chains and led her to a waiting truck.

As she approached the truck, however, Marissa tripped, then tripped again, almost falling. Confused, she tried to step more carefully. Perhaps it was the floor-length burka, or the steel chains that bound her feet. But her head was now swimming. She found it more and more difficult to keep her balance and her vision was beginning to fade.

As the last wisp of consciousness fled from her mind, Marissa realized to her horror that she'd been drugged.

And now she found herself locked in a wooden box, being driven through the desert to be presented as a gift to some mysterious sheikh.

With full realization of her situation, claustrophobia set in. The walls of the box closed in around her. She began pounding against the lid of the box and screaming.

Within minutes, the truck slowed, then pulled to the side of the road. A few minutes more and she heard the lid of the box being unlatched. Finally it swung open.

The light was blinding. Marissa quickly shut her eyes, then slowly blinked them open again as the searing pain behind her eyes gradually eased. She still felt sick.

The ISIS commander named Abdullah was looking at her through the mesh window of her burka. "The drugs have worn off." He told the driver. "But we're through the border checkpoints now. She can ride in the front the rest of the way."

Knowing that her body was still weakened by the drugs, he lifted her from the box and carried her to the front of the truck, placing her upright in the second row of seats and securing the chain that bound her ankles to a metal clasp on the floorboard.

Through the mesh window of the burka, Marissa glanced around, searching for landmarks. She knew that escape from ISIS slavery was sometimes possible. Of the thousands of women captured by ISIS, more than five hundred had escaped to tell their story. But escape would be easier if she knew where she was.

There was not much to see. They were on a narrow, poorly-paved road, driving across a vast desert. Judging by the position of the sun, they were traveling almost due west. Visualizing a map of the Middle East, Marissa was encouraged. *We're headed toward Jordan!*

A moment later she corrected herself. *Abdullah said we've already passed the border checkpoints. That means we are already IN Jordan. We're out of ISIS territory!* She breathed a deep sigh of relief.

After more than an hour, they slowed and turned off the desert road onto what seemed nothing more than a camel track heading off to the left. For two more hours they continued through the desert, heading south into the parched no-man's land between Jordan and Saudi Arabia.

Around evening, they arrived at what appeared to be an old Roman fortress standing in the middle of a small oasis. It was surrounded by dozens of Bedouin tents and a small grove of date palms.

Exiting the truck, the ISIS commander led Marissa through the fort's heavy iron gates and across its dusty courtyard. Torches flickered on the walls.

Passing through another set of iron gates into a dimly-lit chamber, Marissa was startled to see the stainless steel doors of a modern elevator. Abdullah directed her to enter, and they descended several levels.

When the elevator doors opened, Abdullah escorted her into one of the most opulent rooms

Marissa had ever seen.

The place was expansive, with an airy feel, and tastefully decorated. She could scarcely believe they were more than sixty feet beneath the surface of the desert. The floors were of polished marble, accented with beautiful oriental rugs. The walls were marble as well, with gold-trimmed pillars and hung with exquisite tapestries. The doorways to the room were concealed behind ornately embroidered curtains. Most impressive of all, however, was the rush of cool air Marissa felt as she exited the elevator. The place was air conditioned! The cool air was startling after weeks in the unrelenting heat of an Iraqi summer.

"This place is beautiful!" Marissa said softly. *I'm back in civilization! Maybe my nightmare IS about to end!*

Several guards greeted them at the entrance. One of them welcomed Abdullah warmly and added, "The sheikh has been informed of your presence. He will be here momentarily."

Gesturing toward Marissa, the ISIS commander said, "I've brought a gift for the sheikh. A female slave. Please prepare her for his arrival."

The guards led Marissa to the center of the room, well away from any furnishings, removed her chains and her burka, and left her standing naked on a beautiful oriental rug.

Having instructed Marissa to remain in place until the sheikh arrived, the guards returned to the entrance and were soon engaged in an animated conversation with Abdullah. He was describing in graphic detail a raid he'd led on an infidel village. The guards were enthralled by his no-doubt-exaggerated account of the plunder he'd taken, the female slaves he'd captured, and his harrowing escape from American military drones.

Meanwhile, Marissa remained on display in the center of the room, feeling awkward, exposed, and extremely vulnerable. *What am I supposed to be doing?*

Time passed. She looked at the guards in confusion. *No one is paying any attention to me. They're treating me like I'm just a piece of furniture.*

Marissa had intended to take the same defiant stance here that she'd taken in the slave market, but physical exhaustion was taking its toll. She found it more and more difficult just to remain standing. As her weariness increased, she shifted her weight from foot to foot, dug her toes into the soft pile of the rug, and fumbled nervously with her hands.

After what seemed like an eternity, the curtains parted and a massive hulk of a man entered the room. He was dressed simply in a black *thobe*, the ankle-length robe worn by Arab men. On his head he had a white *Keffiyeh*, the traditional middle-eastern headdress, held in place by two circlets of black rope. His beard was long, black, and untrimmed.

Abdullah greeted the sheikh warmly as they kissed each other on the cheek and embraced. They spoke for several minutes, then Abdullah presented Marissa, and the sheikh turned to face her.

For the first time, Marissa had a clear view of the sheikh's face, but she was not prepared for what she saw. His beard could not conceal the fact that his face was horribly scarred and deformed, as though melted by intense heat. Beyond his physical deformity, however, she discerned something else, something she had no words to describe. Marissa sensed that behind the sheikh's ruined countenance, something immensely evil was brooding, something so vile and cruel and sadistic that the very sight of him sent a tremor of revulsion through the core of her being.

As his blood-dark eyes fixed on Marissa, his mouth twisted in a malevolent grin. "Ah... a new plaything for my harem!" he beamed, "Let me see what you've brought me."

The sheik stood back and appraised her. Dark circles surrounded Marissa's eyes. Her usually luxuriant hair was stringy, disheveled and matted with perspiration. Her unclothed body, having gone five days in the desert without bathing, was streaked with dirt and grime — but her beauty could not be concealed.

The sheikh glanced at Abdullah with a knowing smile, "Very good, Abdullah; you know what I like!"

As the huge man drew close to Marissa, her eyes widened and her body trembled involuntarily. She could not take her eyes from his hideous face. Without conscious thought, her quivering lips silently formed a single word, *"wahshan!"* It was the Arabic word for monster.

Reading her lips, the sheikh repeated the word aloud. *"Wahshan?"*

Then he said it again, louder — laughing heartily this time, *"WAHSHAN!* My new plaything has called me a monster. I must show her how perceptive she is!"

He reached out a massive hand and gently grasped the soft flesh between Marissa's shoulder and her neck. She shuddered at his touch. *What is he doing?*

Fixing his eyes intently on hers, the sheikh held his hand in place for a moment, then began slowly massaging her shoulder, moving his fingers slightly, exploring, probing—seeking just the right spot. And finding it, he began to squeeze, steadily increasing the pressure. Marissa winced, and he squeezed even harder. His thumb and forefinger penetrated deep into the yielding tissue, squeezing her shoulder until tears of pain formed in her eyes. Marissa was in agony. She dropped, trembling, to her knees, struggling not to cry out, not taking her eyes from his face.

The sheikh leaned close, his malformed mouth just inches from her ear. "*ANA WAHSHAN!*" he growled softly, "I *am* a monster! A monster such as you have never imagined, not in your worst nightmares. And you will soon discover that fact for yourself!"

As the sheikh released his hold, Marissa's body slumped onto the ornate rug, still trembling from the excruciating pain. Ignoring her agony, the sheikh turned to two of his guards. "Bathe her thoroughly and place her in a cell. I will give her my full attention tomorrow. Tonight I must meet with Abdullah."

As the guards helped her to her feet and led her through richly embroidered curtains to the darkened hallway beyond, two thoughts exploded in Marissa's consciousness.

The first was that her hopes of escaping this citadel had been a fantasy. She knew now she would likely be here for a very long time.

Even before that thought had fully registered, the second thought struck with numbing certainty: Her nightmare was not about to end after all. It had only just begun.

The sheikh and Abdullah watched quietly as Marissa was led from the room. When she had gone, the sheikh turned to the guard standing watch at the entrance, "Abdullah and I will be meeting in my private office. Be sure to show Kareina in, as soon as she arrives."

Chapter Five:
Wedding Plans

THE ISLAND OF IONA

It was Lys who first suggested a double wedding.

With her folks flying over from the states to attend the ceremony, it just made sense to combine her wedding with her brother's. Patrick, Roger, and Jamie all loved the idea. None had ever attended a double wedding, but it seemed like a great plan.

The idea was to do a beach wedding, weather permitting, at *Port Ban*, on the very spot Roger had proposed to Jamie.

A beach wedding sounded like it would be simple to organize, which was good since the date was now only weeks away.

As the plans progressed, however, they soon discovered that an incredible number of details still had to be covered. At first they felt overwhelmed and even considered postponing the wedding. Then Jamie volunteered to organize the event. Using her administrative skills, she soon had lists made up and tasks assigned for each member of the wedding party, as well as for all their volunteer friends.

Just like the song says, Jamie thought, *we'll get by with a little help from our friends!*

Less than a week before the wedding, the Irin called a meeting of the whole synaxis.

The entire Iona Synaxis was there, along with Holmes and Piper, who had flown in for the wedding ceremony, bringing several of Lys's friends from the first synaxis.

The meeting was led by Rand, who arrived in typical Irin fashion, simply appearing in the room, along with Eliel and Araton.

As the group welcomed them, Rand folded her wings back into a dimension where they couldn't be seen, and took a seat in front of the fireplace.

After a few minutes of casual conversation, she began.

"We know everyone's focus is on the wedding right now, and we join you in that excitement. But we *are* at a critical place.

"Before everyone gets too distracted by the wedding plans, I want to give a progress reports on our situation worldwide.

"On the surface, everything is going very well, even better than expected.

"Synaxis groups worldwide now number more than 400, with more being added every month. In areas where they are allowed to operate freely, the groups are spreading exponentially.

"Where synaxis groups can be formed and operate freely, the results are already impressive.

"Crime and terrorism are down. The economy is recovering, bringing whole regions into a new level of prosperity. Several locations have been so freed of Archon oppression, they feel almost like Iona!

"But in countries with repressive regimes it's difficult for synaxis groups to form, and those that do are forced to meet in secret.

"Our concern is that while the enemy is being driven back, they are not leaving. They are consolidating in nations where synaxis groups are less free to operate.

"The result is that a great polarization is taking place.

"Some places, like Iona, feel almost like heaven on earth, but others are becoming more and more like Hades."

"Good is getting more powerful," Eliel cut in. "But evil is operating more openly, and also with greater power."

"So while we are seeing great progress," Rand continued, "we need to understand that the battle is actually intensifying.

"I do believe we will win this, but as we move forward, we can expect some desperate moves on the part of the Archons.

"So even as you prepare for the wedding, be alert. The enemy is out there."

Chapter Six:
The Sheikh and the Djinn

THE SHEIKH'S PALACE – IN THE DESERT OF EASTERN JORDAN

The desert east of Amman, Jordan is an endless expanse of windblown sand and sun-scorched, black basalt rock, extending northward toward Syria, eastward into Iraq, and south into Saudi Arabia.

Stretching incongruously across that vast wasteland is a ragged line of ancient castles. Though mostly in ruins now, they had been built as luxurious pleasure palaces by the Umayyad Caliphs in the seventh century.

The most remote of these desert castles, *Qasr–Al-Wadi*, hails from an even earlier date.

Built as a Roman fort around A.D. 300, *Qasr–Al-Wadi* was originally constructed as a cavalry outpost to keep Arab nomads from attacking caravans laden with frankincense and myrrh.

The fortress was rebuilt in the 7th Century as a pleasure palace for the Umayyad Caliph Al-Warif.

In modern times, it had been rebuilt again by a mysterious Arab billionaire known only as "the sheikh."

In Arab legends, *Qasr–Al-Wadi* also bears the

name, *Qasr-Al-Djinn*, the Stronghold of Demons. Located in a desolate and jagged valley carved out of the desert that spills over from Saudi Arabia, the Bedouin consider it a haunted place, where demons come at night to murder the unsuspecting.

At the foot of *Qasr-Al-Djinn* is a cluster of flat-roofed Bedouin tents, housing the guards that keep watch over the sheikh's palace.

Tonight the men of the encampment are celebrating a feast.

In the middle of the circle of tents, a large open area had been laid out with traditional Arabian carpets, along with low tables and ornate cushions, positioned for seating. A large fire had been kindled in the center of the circle, in preparation for the cold desert night.

One by one, the sheikh's guards took their seats, all dressed in their finest regalia. The meal began with small bowls of olives and nuts, served by shabbily dressed slave girls. The girls, looking weak and mal-nourished, gazed longingly at the food they served, as though they would have loved to sample some of it themselves. None of them seemed older than ten or twelve.

At the far side of the circle, a smaller fire has been kindled. The blackened, iron tea kettle resting on the gently flickering flames, was emitting a faint trail of grey steam.

When the tea was ready, an older slave girl, fourteen or fifteen years old, brought around a silver tray of finger sized glasses. With practiced expertise, she filled each one to the brim with the hot, minty tea, and presented each of the men with a glass.

Music began, and a trio of provocatively dressed belly dancers emerged, gliding among the seated men, their lithe bodies in continual motion, flowing seductively to the beat of the music. Bedouin dancers in long robes joined them, leaping and twirling around the open area. The music reverberated from the fortress walls, as the searing sun dropped below the western hills. As darkness encroached, the air became strongly scented with the smell of hashish.

Near the smaller fire, a raised section of sand had been fenced off with wooden poles. A lantern dangled above it, sending flickers of light across the area. The raised area was an underground oven packed with layers of potatoes, vegetables and slow cooked meats. The food had been placed upon a bed of hot coals the night before, with the sand sealing in the heat.

As the men enjoyed a banquet of Jordanian flat breads, hummus, and herb-infused oils, an old man approached the oven. With a gloved hand, he removed a large cast-iron lid, allowing the glorious aroma of slow roasted meat and seasoned vegetables to spread through the camp.

As the evening progressed, the Bedouin sat around the fire, feasting extravagantly. Their loud voices boomed as they laughed amongst themselves, faces glowing in the shadowy light.

"Did you hear?" one said, "Abdulah returned from the ISIS market two weeks ago with a beautiful new slave girl for the sheikh. He told me that the next time he comes, he'll bring a whole cargo of slaves!"

"Tell him not to give the sheikh *all* the beautiful girls!" one of the guards laughed, "Save one or two for the guards to enjoy!"

"Shut up, you son of a donkey!" another guard cautioned. "You don't want to anger the sheikh!"

After dinner, the festivities continued as the men played drums and sang heartily.

Suddenly, a frigid desert night-wind gusted through the camp and jostled the flames. Something about it sent a chill up the spine of every man there.

A hush fell over the celebration. With a look of terror in their eyes, several guards silently mouthed the words, "The *djinn!*"

To the Bedouin, the arrival of a *djinn*, or desert demon, was always an occasion to fear. The Bedouin believe the *djinn* are malicious beings, come from another realm to bring bad luck, illness, and death. Normally invisible, *djinn* are masterful shape-shifters, and can masquerade as humans, demons, or ghosts. They can also appear in beautiful, seductive forms.

A tall man wearing white, flowing robes and a red and white checkered head scarf rose from his cushion and left the circle of tents to investigate.

The moon had risen, flooding the desert with eerie silver light. Drifted sand glimmered in extended ripples, as if an ocean had suddenly been frozen into immobility.

Leaning forward, straining his eyes into the elusive darkness, the man saw that his fears were confirmed.

Fifty yards east of the camp, a ring of standing

stones lay half buried in sand. In the center of those stones, a whirlwind had formed—a dark storm of swirling sand-wind.

The man called in a loud voice. "It *IS* the *djinn!*"

A man named Mohammad cried out, "It can't be the *djinn.* She was just here two weeks ago!"

"I tell you, it's the *djinn.*" The tall man reiterated as he came back into the circle of tents. "She's come back again. I just saw the whirlwind in the stone circle. She'll be here within moments!"

Most of the men were now on their feet, hurriedly gathering their belongings, but one portly man in a black and white checkered *Keffiyeh* leaned back and laughed. "I don't believe in any *djinn!* Djinn and ghosts are figments of the imagination!"

"You are new here, Farouk!" the tall man chided him. "I once believed as you do, but tonight you will see the *djinn* for yourself. Then you will believe... and fear. But come, it's best to view a *djinn* from a place of concealment."

The feast had suddenly ended. The fire was quickly extinguished and within minutes food was swept away. The men withdrew to their tents and tied down the door flaps.

They stood, peering fearfully through narrow slits, as the dark spectral form of the desert demon passed through their camp to enter the fort.

A guard met Kareina at the elevator door.

"Tell the sheikh I must speak with him immediately."

The guard, attempting to quell the shaking in his knees, bowed, backed away, and ran to get the sheikh.

The sheikh had just come from his harem and was drenched with perspiration.

"The *djinn* has returned!" the trembling servant blurted.

"Tell her I will be there in a moment," the sheikh said as he hurriedly tore off his clothing and ran to the shower.

Within moments, he emerged refreshed, dressed in his finest *thaub*.

Walking nonchalantly through a richly embroidered curtain, his deformed face brightened in a twisted smile.

"Kareina, it's so good to see you again! I wasn't expecting you so soon. It seems like Abdulah and I just met with you two weeks ago."

Unimpressed by the sheikh's feigned obeisance. Kareina spoke directly. "I've come here because I need you to take immediate action.

"I've been reviewing some figures and have great concern — over a third of the terror attacks we've planned in the past four months have failed, and that number is increasing.

"Our strategy has been that your terror networks would so disrupt western civilization that it collapses. That is not happening.

"We know the problem is the synaxis. In many areas of the world, synaxis groups are multiplying rapidly, gaining strength much faster than we anticipated.

"As the synaxis members learn to use their gifts, it becomes harder and harder for our plots to succeed. I estimate that by this time next year, 95 percent of our terror attacks will fail.

"If we are going to use terrorism to bring disruption to the Earth-realm, it must be done immediately. We must do something within the next few weeks that is so massive and so widespread, that it will bring all of human civilization to its knees.

"My plan is this. I need your networks to attack 27 airliners in a single day. The effect of that will be unimaginable. Twenty-seven airliners blown out of the sky! Even if a third of the attacks are thwarted, most will succeed. It will bring worldwide air travel to a permanent halt. The already shaky world economy will be dealt a blow from which it will never recover.

"My plan has been carefully considered, and I'm confident that it will work, but it requires a great deal of coordination. That's your job. It will take the cooperation of every major terrorist group worldwide. I will provide you with a new explosive that can pass undetected through any kind of airport screening.

"My question is, do you have the men to do it?"

"Yes," answered the sheikh confidently. "I have many suicide bombers who have sworn to do anything I ask.

"But I also have a question for you," he came back. "You are asking a great deal, Kareina. What do I get?"

"You want *money?*"

"You know I don't need money!

"There's only one thing I ever want. I want new playthings for my harem.

"The girls in the local Bedouin markets are pathetic. They're sickly and malnourished, sold into slavery because their parents can't afford to feed them. Some of them have not even entered puberty." The sheikh shook his head in disgust. "Most of them don't last a week.

"I get an occasional woman from the ISIS markets in Iraq, but not nearly enough. My harem is virtually empty

"When friend Carrington was alive, he kept me well supplied. Strong, healthy American women, full of spirit, some of them lasted for months!

"And," he added with a twisted smile, "many of them were blondes!"

"Like *her?*"

"Yes, like *her*. That's what I want!"

Kareina was thoughtful for a moment, then her lips tightened in a malicious smile.

"I think I know a blonde that would suit your needs perfectly. She's an attractive, strong, high-spirited American, and she's been a thorn in my side for several years. I believe she may be just what you're looking for.

"Make your plans for the attack. I will bring you your blonde."

Chapter Seven:
Abducted

THE CITY OF OBAN, SCOTLAND

Five days before the wedding, Erin, Lys, and Jamie headed out early in the morning for Oban. They caught the first ferry of the day from Iona to Fionnphort, then followed the now-familiar route across the island of Mull.

The road across Mull was a narrow, winding, one-lane affair. Traversing it meant stopping at times to let sheep cross and pulling the big Hummer over frequently, to allow cars traveling the opposite direction to pass.

Despite the narrow road, Lys loved the drive across Mull. The island was a place of almost surreal beauty, with desolate glens, deep lochs, impassible bogs, and ancient brooding castles. But this day the subject of conversation in the Hummer had nothing to do with the landscape of Mull. The three women were totally focused on the upcoming wedding and of the dozens of details that still needed to be hammered out.

The big issue this morning was wedding photography. The couples had decided to use two different photographers to be sure everything was covered, and had also arranged to video the ceremony. Both photographers had requested lists of the specific shots the couples wanted, and Jamie, of course, had sent a list to her photographer a week ago.

But Lys woke up that morning in a panic, realizing that she'd never emailed her photographer a list. As Erin drove, Lys was frantically typing the list on her iPhone, frequently asking Jamie for advice.

Catching the ferry from Craignure to Oban, their first stop was Oban and the Isles Airport where they dropped off Erin. The Fletcher jet was crewed and waiting to take off when Erin arrived. Erin was taking her private jet back to the states to pick up Lys's parents for the wedding. They were due back in two days.

Erin had volunteered to fly Patrick's folks also, but after a lifetime in the military, stationed in locations all over the world, Patrick's dad had recently retired and fulfilled his life-long dream of moving back to the "old country." Patrick's parents had just purchased a picturesque farmhouse in Northern Ireland and were planning to fly over to Scotland the day before the wedding.

Dropping Erin at the airport, Lys drove into downtown Oban and parked the Hummer near the dressmakers' shop. Today was the final fitting for their wedding gowns, and only a few minor alterations were required. The seamstress told Jamie and Lys they should be able to pick up the gowns in two days.

Perfect timing! Lys thought. *I can get the dresses when I drive over to pick up Erin and my folks. One more item off the check-list!*

The thought of her mom and dad coming to

Iona for her wedding was almost overwhelming to Lys. Her family had always been close, and having her dad "give her away" had been a childhood dream. Lys could hardly wait to see her parents again.

Leaving the dressmaker's shop, Lys let Jamie take the Hummer. Jamie was heading directly back to Iona to meet with Catherine about refreshments for the reception, but Lys had arranged to meet Patrick for lunch at Aidan's Pub, which was just a few blocks away.

Lys glanced at her watch. *I'm running late! I was supposed to meet Patrick at noon.*

Lys declined Jamie's offer to drop her off. "It's so close, I think I can get there quicker walking."

Leaving the dressmakers, Lys chose to take a shortcut through a narrow alleyway, walking fast, almost running. She hated the thought of keeping Patrick waiting.

Halfway down the alley, a jogger dressed in black came up beside her and matched her pace. Something about him made her feel extremely uncomfortable.

Glancing at the man, Lys couldn't shake the feeling that there was something familiar about him. Then she realized who he was. The jogger was Grat Dalton. Lys had only seen him once before. It had been on her first visit to Oban, when she'd sheltered a terrified Erin Vanderberg on a busy Oban street. Erin's former husband Rex had just come out of a pub and was loudly joking with Grat about how they would torture and kill Erin when they found her.

Grat Dalton's was not a face Lys could easily

forget. Seeing him made her blood run cold. *What the hell is he doing here?*

Before Lys could react to Grat's presence, however, a delivery van pulled up next to her with a loud screech of brakes as its side door rumbled open.

Glancing at the van in surprise, Lys was not prepared for what happened next. The moment the van door opened, Grat lunged at her from behind, clamping one hand firmly over her mouth and another grasping her waist. His momentum carried both of them through the van door where two sets of hands grasped them and pulled them in, as the door slid shut. The van was already in motion. The whole thing had taken less than ten seconds.

Looking around in confusion in the darkness of the van, Lys saw a figure crouched in the back. It was a tall, plain-faced woman with long black hair. In a flash of recognition, Lys gasped, *"Kareina!"*

Chapter Eight:
The Search for Lys

AIDEN'S PUB, THE CITY OF OBAN

Aidan's was a quintessential Scottish pub. Its well-stocked bar was situated prominently in the center of the establishment, with the taproom on one side and a cozy dining room on the other. The surrounding walls were awash with maritime prints, honoring Oban's centuries-long seafaring heritage.

Patrick and Lys had always loved Aidan's warmth and charm. The place also brought back many memories. Patrick and Lys, along with several other members of the original synaxis, had eaten at Aidan's on their first visit to Oban.

It had also been the site of Derek and Piper's wedding reception. Locals still hotly debate what really happened when Holmes and Piper left for their honeymoon by apparently disappearing into thin air.

Patrick sat at a table near the back of the dining room, waiting for Lys. She'd been supposed to meet him at noon, but he was not surprised that she was running late.

She'd spent the morning with Jamie doing last minute wedding preparations and they'd probably lost track of time in their excitement. He ordered an appetizer and nibbled on it while he waited for Lys to arrive.

Time went by.

When he finished the appetizer, he began to be concerned.

At twelve-thirty he tried texting her, but the text did not go through.

He attempted to call her, but the call went straight to voicemail. *That's strange. Her phone must be turned off. That's not like Lys.*

He finally decided to call Jamie.

"Hey, Jamie, where are you?"

"Hi, Patrick. I just drove off the ferry on Mull. I'm on my way back to Iona."

"Is Lys with you?"

"No, I left her in Oban. She said she was meeting you for lunch."

"How long ago was that?"

Jamie glanced at her watch. "It was almost an hour ago. Is something wrong?"

Patrick was beginning to feel a cold weight in the pit of his stomach, and he knew it was not the appetizer. "Lys never showed up. I've been waiting here at Aidan's since before noon.

"My texts don't go through and she's not answering her phone. I'm sure there are plenty of perfectly harmless explanations, but I'm beginning to be concerned. I'll wait for her here for another half-hour, then try driving around Oban to see if I can see anything of her.

"When you get to Iona, would you check to see if any of the Irin have heard anything?"

Patrick spent an hour driving the streets of

Oban, but never found Lys.

As he returned to Iona, a sense of dread gripped him. Lys was not only his fiancée, she was his best friend. He'd already faced the possibility of losing her when she'd entered Hades to rescue Jamie. Patrick could not bear the thought of losing her again.

Patrick had asked Jamie to arrange for Araton, Rand, and Eliel to meet him at Iona House at four. When he got there, he found that most of the Iona synaxis had shown up as well.

As Patrick explained what had happened, they all were clearly distressed. There had still been no word from Lys.

"We'll use all our resources to find her." Araton promised.

Over the next two hours, several dozen Irin spread out through the shadow realm and searched the city of Oban, but could find no trace of Lys.

That night at seven, they met together in Iona House with the rest of the synaxis.

Michael said, "The last time Lys disappeared in Oban, she'd been kidnapped by Kareina. I hate to say it, but something like that seems more and more a possibility.

"With the Archon's ability to access the shadow realm, they could have taken her anywhere in the world by this time. Or back to Hades."

"Isn't there any way to locate her?" Catherine asked.

"I have an idea." Roger said, turning to Jamie. "How's that new computer network coming?"

"We have 426 synaxis groups already connected. It's 95 percent operational. We might miss a few, but we can contact almost every synaxis on earth, instantly."

"Here's my idea for finding Lys. Almost every synaxis has at least one person with the second-sight gift. They can 'see beyond,' viewing levels of reality our natural senses are blind to, sometimes even sensing events before they happen.

"Many of the synaxis members are still immature in their gifts, and can't yet use their gifts with full accuracy, but with over 400 groups we should have a fair number that can.

Michael immediately saw what Roger was thinking. "Roger, you're a genius! I think that might work!

"Jamie, contact all the groups in the network and ask them to have their people meet together in an emergency synaxis. Have everyone with the second-sight gift try to discern what they can about Lys.

"Ask them to communicate back to us what they see... and do it quickly.

"Lys literally saved our world by opening the Iona portal. It's our turn to save her."

"I'll get the word out right now," Jamie said, pulling out her laptop. "Given the number of time zones involved and the time it will take for some of the groups to gather their members, it might be a while before we get a significant number of responses. Why don't we meet back here at 6 AM and see what we've learned?"

Patrick slept little that night. The situation reminded him so much of the vigil at Loch Buie. He'd paced the area around the Loch Buie portal for days, anxious for something to happen, not knowing if he'd ever see Lys again.

He left Iona House and went for a walk on the moonlit beach . Patrick had the second-sight gift, but his emotions were in such turmoil he couldn't be sure what he was seeing. One recurring vision was of a jail cell set in a large room full of strange looking objects.

Glancing at his watch he saw that it was now past midnight. *Only four days till the wedding! Where are you Lys?*

At 6 AM the synaxis met together with a number of Irin in the main living area of Iona House.

Jamie had been up most of the night, collecting and collating the reports that came in and conferring with Rand.

Every eye turned to Jamie as she began to speak.

"Over 60 percent of the synaxis groups have now reported back, and a fair number reported at least some measure of success in locating Lys.

"Unfortunately, we've got good news and bad news.

"The first piece of good news is: we now know exactly where Lys is.

"The next piece of good news is that no one saw her in Hades. She's still here on planet earth."

Holding a sheaf of papers in her right hand, she said, "It's interesting to see what we've come up with."

"47 saw her in the middle-east.

"16 pinpointed her in a desert region between Jordan and Saudi Arabia.

"6 saw her in locked in a cell in an underground bunker.

"3 actually gave map coordinates.

"So the good news is that Lis is still in the Earth-realm, and we know exactly where she is.

"Now for the bad news. I've talked to Rand and learned that the location where Lys is now imprisoned is a known Archon stronghold and has been for generations. It's presently the location of the underground fortress of a terrorist mastermind who calls himself the sheikh. The man is a psycho who gets his kicks by torturing women, so Lys may be in serious trouble."

"But there's even more bad news." Jamie hesitated, glancing at Rand. "Rand, would you like to explain the situation?

"The worst news of all," Rand said, "is that the place is so heavily guarded that the Irin can't approach it. In the shadow realm there are literally thousands of Archon warriors guarding the sheikh's portal. We believe this place must be crucial to their current plans, and they are not about to let it be taken.

"Which means," Rand said, "there's no way we can reach Lys."

"Wait a minute!" Michael cut in, "I'm getting a serious sense of *déjà vu* here! I mean, haven't we had this conversation before?

"We all heard how impregnable Hades was, and how no one could enter Abadon to rescue Jamie.

Yet Roger, Lys and I went into Hades and rescued her! It was not easy, but we found a way.

"Why can't some of our synaxis members infiltrate this place and find Lys?"

Rand was silent for a moment, then answered. "Believe it or not, this place is much more difficult than Hades ever was, and for several reasons.

"One reason you succeeded in Hades was because Hades was not heavily defended. There were no military patrols. The portal was unguarded. No one ever expected anyone to try to break into Hell. It was only by accident that you were spotted at all.

"Beyond that, you had the advantage of being able to blend in with Abadon's sizable slave population.

"None of that would be true here. You would stick out like the proverbial sore thumb among the sheikh's Bedouin guards.

"But not only is the sheikh's stronghold protected by Archons. Beneath the deceptive façade of an ancient Roman fortress, the place is a highly secure military facility. The sheikh's actual palace is located sixty feet underground, protected by yards of reinforced concrete. An A-bomb could go off at the surface and not penetrate.

"In short, Lys is in a very bad place. We need to face the fact that she may not survive. But at the present time, there's not a damn thing we can do about it!"

"But we *have* to do something!" Michael insisted.

"Look," Rand said, glaring at Michael in

obvious frustration. She seemed almost at the point of tears. "When I say this cannot be done, I'm not saying it lightly! I've come to know Lys as a friend. Eliel and I are both supposed to be in her wedding. If there was *anything* I could do to save her I would do it. I'd lay down my life for her if I thought it would help. But it would *not* help. Believe me, I've looked at the facts. There's literally nothing we can do!"

Finally another voice spoke, "I can rescue her."

As everyone turned to look, the speaker continued, "You are right that none of the synaxis members could succeed in rescuing Lys, however badly they want to.

"I also agree that none of the Irin would survive an attempt.

"But Lys must still be rescued.

"As a few of the Irin know, I *have* the ability to do this. I know the risk is great, but I have the ability and I *must* rescue Lys, no matter what the consequences."

Chapter Nine:
In the Monster's Lair

THE SHEIKH'S PALACE - DEEP
IN THE ARABIAN DESERT

Lys stirred slowly, blinking her eyes open, trying to figure out where she was. Vague pictures of the kidnapping flashed in her mind. The last thing she remembered was watching Kareina plunge a hypodermic needle into her thigh.

Where am I?

Lys glanced around, trying to make sense of what she was seeing.

She appeared to be in a large cage or prison cell. Iron bars made up three of the walls, with a solid slab of concrete for the fourth. The top of the cage, more than ten feet high, was closed in by iron bars as well. There were no furnishings of any kind. *Not the most luxurious of accommodations!*

Another realization hit. *They've taken my clothing!* She was lying stark naked on a bare concrete floor.

Pulling herself into a sitting position, Lys saw that her cell was one of six identical cells aligned against one wall of a huge, dimly-lit room. The cell next to hers was the only other occupied cell, but the woman there — also naked — appeared to be unconscious.

The rest of the cavernous chamber looked like something from a horror movie.

A darkened ceiling arched more than twenty feet overhead and was festooned with thick iron chains, winches, and pulleys. On the far wall stood a large electrical transformer, from which led clusters of red and black high-voltage cables. Arranged around the room were smaller cages in various shapes and sizes, some resting on the floor, with others suspended from the ceiling. Rows of manacles dangled from the walls at various heights. Near the center of the room she saw what appeared to be an inclined operating table with shackles fixed at its head and foot.

Lys knew immediately what the room was. Though she had never seen one, there was no doubt in her mind. This was a torture chamber.

Her revulsion increased as she continued to scan the room. She rose to her feet and clutched the bars of her cell door, trying to envision the unspeakable acts that must have occurred in this place of horror. Though she could only guess what some of the objects were used for, it was clear that the room was filled with implements of torture of every kind.

From the multitude of blood stains on the floor and the pervasive stench of decaying flesh, she knew this room had seen a great deal of use, and recently.

Hearing Lys stirring, the woman in the next cell rolled over to face her. "Welcome to Hell," she said weakly.

"I've already been to Hell," Lys answered.

"Been there, done that, don't want the T-shirt." Then glancing around the room one more time, she added, "This does look a lot like Hell though... What *is* this place?"

The woman slowly eased herself into a sitting position, leaning against the solid concrete wall at the back of her cell.

"This is the personal pleasure palace of a man they call the sheikh," she said. "He sometimes calls this room his harem. He also calls it his playroom. In reality, it's a torture chamber where he molests and abuses women.

"You're his newest plaything, to put it bluntly."

The woman looked at Lys with genuine sympathy. "I heard the guards talking about you when they brought you in last night. I don't know who you are but I've got to tell you, your future is not looking bright."

Lys gripped the iron bars of the cell's door more firmly and tried shaking it. It did not budge.

She tried again, using all her strength. "I've got to get out of here." Lys gritted her teeth in frustration. "I'm getting married in four days."

"I hate to tell you this honey, but that's probably not going to happen. The sheikh's palace is an underground fortress. We're at least 60 feet beneath the surface of the earth in a remote section of Arabian Desert. I doubt the US marines could spring you from this place."

"Who is this sheikh?"

"He's your worst nightmare," the woman

responded. "A true monster. He's also the mind behind most of the terror attacks worldwide in the last thirty years."

"He's a terrorist?"

"He doesn't participate in any of the attacks himself, but he's behind almost all of them.

"I've learned a lot about terror networks since I've been here. The groups you hear about in the news — groups like Al-Qaeda, ISIS, Al Shabaab, and Boko Haram — are like the arms of an octopus. The sheikh is their head. He's the mastermind. From this remote underground complex, he provides resources, strategy, and direction for all of them.

"Of course, I doubt the sheikh has the mental capacity to mastermind much of anything himself. He's just a figurehead. The real direction comes from a mysterious woman named Kareina. He calls her his spirit-guide. I've only seen her once. The Arabs here are terrified of her. They say she's a *djinn*, a desert spirit.

"When the sheikh is not carrying out Kareina's instructions, his mental energy is consumed with just one thing, and that's the torture of women. It's his passion, and he considers himself an expert."

"Has he tortured you?"

"Repeatedly. He comes down here two or three times a day. Sometimes briefly. Sometimes for hours at a time. He beats me, tortures me, sometimes he rapes me, but one thing he has not done — he has not yet broken me. And that frustrates the hell out of him. But he keeps trying. I don't know how much longer I can hold out."

Lys looked at her prison-mate with new compassion. She was an attractive woman, but looked haggard and weary. Multiple overlapping bruises bore silent witness to the torment she'd endured.

"By the way," Lys said, "my name's Lys Johnston."

"Pleased to meet you, Lys, though I'm sorry it has to be under these circumstances. I'm Marissa Kobani.

"Believe it or not, I'm a medical doctor with the World Health Organization. Until a few weeks ago I was heading up a medical relief team in northern Iraq."

"How did you get *here?*"

Marissa briefly recounted her story, beginning with the ISIS raid on the village of Erba Abdol, and ending in the sheikh's dungeon of horror.

Lys listened with mounting dismay as Marissa described the carnage in the village, the plight of the captured Yazidi women and the scene at the Islamic State's slave market.

"You're right, Marissa," Lys said finally. "This *is* Hell.

"Hell has come to earth. This is what the Archons want for our whole planet."

"Who are the Archons?"

"That's what Kareina is. I know all about Kareina. She's tried to kill me several times. She's bad news.

"But what about this sheikh?" Lys asked. "What do you know about him?"

Marissa was silent for a moment, then finally

spoke, "Most of the guards here won't talk to me. I'm the sheikh's personal plaything, and any guard that shows an interest in me would end up in the torture chamber himself. So most of them won't even make eye contact.

"But the servant who brings me my meals loves to talk. He sits and babbles while I eat. I've learned quite a bit from him.

"He says the sheikh was a member of the royal family of a wealthy middle-eastern kingdom. His father was one of the richest men in the world. But when the sheikh was twelve years old, his home was destroyed in a terrible fire. His mother and younger brothers were burned to death and the sheikh was horribly scarred.

"His distraught father called in the best plastic surgeons in the world, but they could do little to help his son's appearance.

"His father did his best to comfort him. Not wanting him to know the horror of his true appearance, his father banned mirrors from his residence. Private tutors were hired to educate him so he never spent time with other teenagers. As the boy grew into his mid-teens, the father hired beautiful young prostitutes to cater to his son's every whim. The result was entirely predictable. In spite of horrible disfigurement, the sheikh grew up believing he was irresistibly attractive to women.

"When he turned eighteen, he enrolled in a university in the States. It was there he learned the truth.

"During his first months in America, the young

man was shocked to find that every girl he met was utterly repulsed by his appearance. For the first time in his life, he experienced rejection, ridicule, and even open contempt. He was at first shocked, then angered, and finally outraged.

"There was one girl in particular... He never mentions her name, I'm not sure he even knows it. He just calls her 'her.' She was evidently a popular girl on campus, slender and athletic with long blonde hair—a cheerleader for the school's football team.

"The sheikh was smitten with her. As days passed, he became obsessed with her. He wanted her like he'd never wanted any woman.

"After weeks of hesitation, he made his move. Summoning his courage, he walked up to her in the university cafeteria, and in front of a table-full of her friends, invited her to his apartment to have sex.

"Assuming it was a joke, the girl laughed at him.

"The sheikh was taken aback by her response, but was not ready to accept rejection.

"Having virtually no social skills, he pressed his case, explaining that he was of royal blood and incredibly wealthy. He offered her a thousand dollars just to sleep with him for one night.

"Repulsed by the blatant proposition, the woman laughed again, mocking him publically and ridiculing his deformity. Then she warned him to stay away from her.

"Still he persisted. Desperate to win her over, he pleaded with her to reconsider, offering her expensive jewelry, a new car, anything she wanted.

"Rather than yielding to his appeal, the outraged young woman stood up in the middle of the cafeteria, screamed profanities at him and threatened to call the police.

"As he fled from the cafeteria in utter humiliation, the raucous laughter of her friends filled the room. It was the most traumatic moment of his life.

"He followed the girl home, and that night broke into her apartment. He found her in bed, having passionate sex with her boyfriend. In a fit of blind rage, the sheikh drew his dagger and decapitated the man where he lay. He then spent an hour torturing the girl to death.

"Responding to her shrieks, the neighbors called the police, but the sheikh escaped from her apartment just as they arrived.

"To avoid an international scandal, his nation's embassy secreted him from the country and tried to cover up the incident, but his father was furious that the family name had been dishonored. The father cut short a business trip to China and flew home to deal with his wayward son. On the way however, the father's jet crashed, leaving no survivors.

"The incident left the sheikh as the sole heir to his family's vast fortune. It also left him with an intense hatred for America, along with all of her infidel allies, as the place of his unforgivable humiliation.

"Unfortunately for you and me, Lys, it also left him with an all-consuming hatred for women.

"I believe torturing the cheerleader to death

was an orgasmic experience for the sheikh and he relives that experience with every new victim. Every woman he molests he compares to her. In his deranged mind, every woman he tortures *is* her. When his playthings inevitably die, he sees himself with her again as the life drains from her body. The monster has spent most of his life venting his unquenchable hatred for that one girl."

Marissa was silent for a moment, the spoke again. "I hate to say it, Lys, but that means he probably has some very special plans for you. From the descriptions I've heard, you look a lot like her."

Chapter Ten: Torture

THE SHEIKH'S PALACE - DEEP
IN THE ARABIAN DESERT

There was a loud, metallic clunk. The door at the end of the chamber swung open and the sheikh entered, accompanied by two guards.

Even though Marissa had warned her, Lys was not prepared for the sheikh. His visage was more than just disfigured. It looked twisted, scarred, and corroded, as though burned by intense heat. Worst of all, Lys sensed that his hideous face was merely a reflection of a far more grotesque mind. The man truly was a monster.

"Good morning, my lovely pets!" the sheikh said in mock cheerfulness, "I'm sorry to be late today, but I had another meeting with Kareina. To make it up to you, I've brought you a special treat.

"In addition to my latest plaything," he said, glancing at Lys for a long moment with obvious delight, "Kareina has given me a wonderful gift. This little bauble!"

He held up a small copper rod with a blue glowing tip.

Lys looked at it with horror. She recognized it immediately. It was a torture implement of Archon manufacture. Her one experience with it had been at the hands of the slave master in the city of Abadon. It had undoubtedly been the most painful experience of her life. Hewett had later explained that the rod operated by nerve induction, hyperstimulating a victim's nervous system to produce excruciating pain, yet causing no real physical damage.

The sheikh walked to the door of Marissa's cell. She was still sitting against the wall at the back of the chamber. "The marvels of technology!" he smiled, holding up the rod again for her to see. "Kareina tells me this little bauble will make every piece of equipment in this room obsolete."

He gestured toward Marissa's cell door. One of the guards unlocked it and swung it open.

"Marissa, my pet, you are about to be the subject of a grand experiment. Since I'm already familiar with your pain response, I've chosen you to be the first woman on earth to sample the effects of my new toy."

The monster glanced at Lys again, then back to Marissa. "The bodies of beautiful women are all very much the same. Did you know they all contain exactly 206 bones? Each of your bodies has approximately 40 pounds of muscle, 25 pounds of fat, 9 pints of blood, and 27 feet of intestine, all enclosed in 14 square feet of soft, pliable skin. The overall package can be very pleasing to the eye, but it is also quite vulnerable.

"I've found many ways to harm a woman. Many ways to cause pain," he sighed. "My problem has been that my pets always expire too quickly.

"Inflicting pain often does irreparable damage to a woman's body. My playthings wear out before I intended—I've lost so many over the years! Within a few short weeks their bodies become too badly broken for them to live.

"But this," he said, looking at the copper rod, "This can change everything!

"Kareina assures me that this rod can inflict undreamed-of levels of pain while doing no harm at all to your lovely bodies. I can play my little games with you week after week, month after month, perhaps even year after year, and your bodies will be none the worse for wear!"

As the sheikh approached her, Marissa's eyes widened. She inched backward, pressing herself tightly against the concrete wall. The guards stood on either side but did not touch her. The sheikh gazed at her longingly for a moment, then reached out his hand and lightly tapped the tip of the rod against her arm.

The response was immediate. At the touch of the copper rod, Marissa's whole body convulsed violently. She screamed and crumpled to the floor, gripping her arm and crying in anguish.

"Exquisite!" The sheikh beamed. "I've never seen a greater pain response than that in any woman!"

Taking his experiment a step further, he reached down and pressed the rod firmly into the soft flesh of Marissa's right thigh, producing an even more devastating effect.

The sheikh stood over her for a moment, watching Marissa writhing in pain on the cell floor. Marissa had finally broken. She could no longer put on a brave front in the face of such unbelievable agony. She began to whimper, and then sob.

"Look!" The sheikh said to the guards. "It didn't even leave a mark! No physical damage! Marissa, my pet, you and I will have such great fun with this in the months to come.

"But I must not neglect my new plaything!" He turned to Lys again and appraised her for a moment.

"Kareina was right," the monster finally said. "You look so much like *her*. I'm going to enjoy this more than you could imagine.

"She was my first... my very first, and it was eminently satisfying. But I was so inexperienced. My methods were crude and destructive — she lasted less than an hour. I've always regretted that. She deserved so much more suffering than I was able to give." He paused a moment, grinning as he held up the copper rod, "But that will not be a problem for us this time!"

As the guards opened her cell door, Lys backed into the far corner, but there was no escaping. The sheikh's men seized her arms and held her immobile.

Entering her cell, the sheikh continued, "Kareina tells me you are in league with the Irin. Perhaps you are hoping they will come to your rescue. Let me assure you that our portal here is so well defended that any Irin who came through would be instantly destroyed. This is the most secure Archon stronghold on earth."

He approached Lys and extended the rod toward her body. He was deliberately moving slowly, watching the mounting terror in her eyes.

Lys pressed her body further back into the

corner of the cell, struggling to distance herself from the inevitable. The guards tightened their grip on her arms.

When the rod's glowing tip was just inches from her torso, the monster paused, as though trying to decide where to apply it first.

Marissa was now crying loudly. She had not prayed in years, but she was praying now in desperation. "Please God, please help us!"

Lys tensed her body, trying to steel herself for unimaginable torment.

But as the monster was about to make his move, a brilliant flash of light illuminated the chamber.

The sheikh froze in place, glancing around the cell, not sure what had happened. Then he saw it.

With the dazzling burst of light, a being had appeared in the cell; a being like nothing he had ever seen. It was human in size and general form, but appeared to be clothed in a brilliant golden light, almost too bright to look at directly. Within the golden glow, what appeared to be beautiful multi-colored flames were in constant motion, shifting in kaleidoscopic patterns across and around its body.

For a moment, both the sheikh and Lys stood transfixed, mesmerized by the awesome apparition.

What IS that? It's not like any Irin I've ever seen. But it's certainly not an Archon!

The air in the cell crackled with energy. In its right hand, the being held a sword that glistened with golden light.

Terrified, the sheikh backed away.

The being spoke to the guards, "Release her!"

When the guards hesitated, the being swung the shining sword in their direction. Something like ball lightning shot down the length of the sword and hit first one, and then the other guard in the chest. With a cry of anguish the guards released Lys and fell to the ground. Fire was consuming their bodies from within. Within moments, nothing remained but ash.

The being then took the sword and slashed it through the air. With a deep, resonant hum, the air parted, creating a rift in the atmosphere—a ragged, brilliantly-glowing ribbon of energy, surrounding a tunnel of total darkness. The rift hung suspended in mid-air in the center of the cell.

The being glanced around for the sheikh, but the monster had fled the chamber.

It turned to Lys. "Come with me."

Lys's eyes were fixed on the glowing rift hovering in the air, just feet away. Was it a portal? It was like no portal she had ever seen. She was terrified at the thought of going through the rift with this mysterious being, but even more terrified at the prospect of staying in the sheikh's dungeon.

"Where are you taking me?" she asked tentatively

The being spoke just one word, but it was the one word she had longed to hear. *"Iona."*

Lys glanced at the next cell. "Marissa! We can't leave her here!"

"Bring her then, but *quickly!*"

Rushing to Marissa's cell, Lys helped her to her

feet. Marissa was still trembling from the excruciating pain, breathing in ragged gasps, but with Lys's help she was able to walk.

The golden being pointed his sword at the gaping hole.

"We must go *now*."

After a moment's hesitation, Lys stepped into the rift. Marissa, too shaken to object, followed her lead.

And suddenly they were in another place.

It was early morning. The sun was already shining brightly. Lys squinted her eyes for a moment against the light.

And then she saw where she was. She was standing on the white sand beach of *Traigh Ban*, right behind Iona House. The morning sunlight sparkled on the Sound of Iona. Gathered around them were the members of the Iona Synaxis, along with twenty or thirty Irin warriors.

Within moments, the whole group converged on Lys and Marissa. Seeing the women emerge from the rift stark-naked, Jamie was already running to the house to fetch bathrobes.

But Patrick was oblivious. With tears of joy streaming down his face, he ran to Lys and threw his arms around her, sweeping her off her feet and squeezing her tightly.

Lys returned the embrace with even greater passion. As Patrick approached, she threw herself into his arms, clinging to him with sobs of joy and relief, holding him like she'd never let him go.

When the two finally released their hold, Jamie

handed Patrick a robe, which he lovingly wrapped around Lys, while Jamie helped Marissa with the other.

Then the rest of the group pressed in, hugging Lys and welcoming Marissa warmly. Though no one in the group knew Marissa, it was clear from her physical condition that she had also been rescued from dreadful torment.

When the initial rush of celebration ended, Marissa—still barely able to stand—collapsed to the sand weeping, thankful that her long nightmare had finally ended.

Through all the celebration, Lys's attention remained focused on her rescuer. The rip in the air had closed, but the being remained standing in front of her, just feet away, clothed in golden light. Whatever this being was, it was far more powerful than any Irin.

Who are you? What are you?

The golden light began to fade. Then suddenly, as if a switch had been flipped, the light dissipated.

The being standing before her now had the form of an ordinary human being.

Lys stood, staring at him, uncomprehending.

Her lips formed two words, "Roger *Dodger?*"

He smiled broadly, "hi, Sis."

There could be no doubt. The mysterious being who had opened a rift in the atmosphere and rescued her from the sheikh's dungeon, was her brother, Roger Johnston.

Chapter Eleven: Roger's Revelation

IONA HOUSE – THE ISLAND OF IONA

Patrick and Lys led Marissa up to the house and let her rest, while Casey and Catherine fixed food for both women. By the time they'd finished eating, Jamie had scrounged some clothing that fit Marissa and gave her time to shower and change.

Every movement Marissa made seemed painful. She moved slowly and with hesitation, wincing occasionally, her whole body trembling. Finally she ventured, "Do you have anything for pain?"

"Yes," Lys responded. "Nothing prescription unfortunately, but we do have some over-the-counter meds. Let me get you some."

As Marissa downed two of the strongest pain-killers they could find, Eliel and Piper came in.

Catherine, Jamie, Eliel, and Piper gathered with Patrick, Lys, and Marissa in the main living area. Lys introduced everyone.

Marissa still appeared nervous and uneasy, and it was obvious that the over-the-counter pain reliever was doing little to ease her suffering.

"We have something else that should help with your pain," Lys began. "Eliel and Piper have quite a track record as healers. Jamie and I have both experienced some remarkable healings. Would you mind them giving it a try?"

Marissa was tempted to roll her eyes, but decided that at this point she'd try anything. "Sure, go ahead," she said, though without much enthusiasm.

Lys gestured to Eliel, who directed Marissa to sit on a comfortable chair they'd placed in the middle of the room. They all gathered around her.

"Tell us what happened to you," said Eliel.

Marissa briefly related her experience in the sheikh's playroom.

Then Eliel told her to relax, and called on the Presence to come. Almost immediately, the familiar sense of the Presence filled the room.

Marissa reacted with surprise as she sensed the Presence for the first time, but quickly relaxed and allowed the gentle sense of the Presence to penetrate her body.

Eliel stood behind Marissa with her hands resting lightly on Marissa's shoulders.

"What do you sense?" Piper asked.

Eliel was silent for a moment, as though in deep concentration. Finally she spoke, "Physically, Marissa has been through a lot. She has three cracked ribs... plus bruising and inflammation of a number of internal organs... nothing life-threatening at this point, but enough to keep her in pretty much constant pain.

"Emotionally, her innate strength has preserved her from a lot of injury, but that last bout with the Archon torture implement has definitely left some scaring."

As Eliel and Piper had done for Jamie just a few weeks earlier, they began with Marissa's physical injuries. Eliel stood back and allowed Piper to lay her hands on Marissa's back, directing her to place them on specific locations. There was a sense of tingling, of energy flowing. The Presence was resting on Marissa in great power.

As she closed her eyes, her breathing deepened. Her body trembled again, but not in pain. Finally she opened her eyes.

"How are you feeling?"

"Much better... thank you!" Marissa smiled in amazement.

She tried moving her body in different ways, obviously pleased to be free of the pain.

"I don't know what you just did, but it was wonderful. I've never experienced anything like that."

She tried standing up, tentatively stretching her body in new directions. Finally she said, "What you did was really strange, but it *worked!* Even my broken ribs feel like they are healed! I feel better than I have in weeks."

"We're not finished yet," Piper said gently. "Please sit back down."

Eliel directed Catherine and Lys to exercise their gifts. Lys sang first, then Catherine joined in. As they sang, the Presence returned, even more strongly this time, releasing healing and wholeness to Marissa's wounded emotions. No longer fearful,

Marissa quickly relaxed and welcomed the Presence.

Marissa had entered the room with her body quaking, eyes darting like a frightened animal. By the time they had finished, she was at peace. She rose and embraced Lys and Catherine, then Eliel and Piper, and with tears rolling down her cheeks, thanking them profusely.

Then, glancing around the room, she said, "But now I have several million questions! Who *are* you people? What is this place? And who the hell was that glowing man with the sword that brought us here?"

Taking their seats again they tried to answer her questions, explaining the ongoing warfare between the Irin and the Archons, and how the synaxis functioned.

Finally Lys added, "As for the glowing man with the sword, we have some questions about him ourselves. Hopefully those questions will be answered tonight."

That evening, the entire synaxis met together in the spacious main living area. Marissa, now thoroughly recovered, had requested permission to come as well.

Every eye was on Roger. They'd all heard the story of what Roger had done to save Lys. All rejoiced in her rescue, but they were also all hungry for an explanation.

Jamie was especially quiet, looking at Roger with uncertainty. *Who is this man? What is he? I'm supposed to marry him in four days, but right now I'm not sure that he really is Roger… or even human!*

Roger looked around the room, and then directly at Jamie. Seeming to read her thoughts, he said, "I guess it's time I explained some things."

The place quieted.

"When I came back from Hi-Ouranos," he began, "the big question in everyone's mind was, 'Is Roger Johnston still the same person?'

"The answer to that is an emphatic, *yes*. This is still my body, down to the last mole, hair, and scar. I don't know how it was translated to Hi-Ouranos from the dragonfire of Hades, but it was. Apart from being in perfect health, my bodily functions are the same as they were before. I have the same thoughts, the same feelings, and the same knowledge. In every way that counts, I'm the same person I was before I went to Hades.

"But a change did take place. When I met with the High King, He did something to me. I can't really describe what it was. I was not fully aware of how much time was passing, but I believe it happened fairly quickly.

"Afterward, there was a new alertness, a sharpening of the senses, a feeling of incredible joy and well-being.

"Then my gifts activated. Not slowly, one-by-one, as you normally see in a synaxis. They were all just *there*, fully functioning. Gifts I had never imagined.

"It was a little confusing at first. A lot of the time I spent in Hi-Ouranos I was being trained to use those new abilities.

"The High King described what happened to me in one word. He said, 'This is the Restoration.'

"He told me that what he had done to me was to fully reverse the damage done to the human race in the great wars.

"Then He told me about the great wars.

"He said the human race, at one time, had been very different from what we've known. The human race had been the highest of all races. It was once common for ordinary men and women to exercise powers we would now call supernatural. Sickness never occurred, and injuries were quickly healed. As with some of the other races in the inhabited worlds, a normal lifespan could stretch to hundreds of thousands of years.

"But 20,000 years ago, the ruler of Hades set out to conquer the other worlds and establish himself as supreme lord.

"He began by invading the Earth-realm. The devastation was unimaginable.

"While humans had much greater power than the Archons individually, the Archon's strength was in their technology.

"Using their biotechnology, they created artificial life forms. That was the first wave of attack. Many of the mythical monsters of human legend, harpies, manticores, gorgons, gryphons, chimeras and many others were actually Archon inventions sent into our world to wreak havoc. Hordes of them came, led by dragons from Hades and hybrid earth-born monsters called Nephilim, swarming through the cities of earth.

"The Archons also had a powerful technology that used sound waves to soften and shift the earth's tectonic plates. They induced great earthquakes. Whole continents slid into the sea. Others were raised up. It was from that era that our legends of Atlantis and the great flood were born. Our race was decimated.

"The worst part of it for us, however, was the Archon ability in the area of genetics. The Archons inflicted terrible genetic damage on our entire race.

"In the midst of the war, they created a virus. It was transmitted through the shadow realm by the artificial life forms we know today as the shades. The presence of the virus was not recognized until it was too late. Every human being had become infected. As a result of this infection, our lifespan was drastically shortened and our life-force nearly extinguished. We lost the ability to use many of our abilities, and our world was opened to invasion.

"In the midst of the destruction, our leaders appealed for help. The few human princes still able to travel between worlds made a heroic journey to Hi-Ouranos to appeal for assistance. The Ancient Ones responded to their appeal and raised up a force to stop the invasion.

"A massive portal was constructed on what is now England's Salisbury Plain, and tens of thousands of volunteers from every inhabited world poured through.

"In a bitterly contested battle, the Archon advance was weakened, but the Archons refused to retreat. Finally, the Ancient Ones authorized a direct assault on Hades.

"After nearly a thousand years of fighting, the armies of Hades were vanquished. It was a time of great horror. Archon civilization collapsed. The inhabitants of Abadon, their one remaining city, burrowed into the remains of an extinct volcano and established a new Archon culture based on their hatred of the human race.

"In their twisted way of thinking, the Archons blame the human race for the destruction of their world. That's why they're still intent on invading our world and taking it for their own.

"But the High King decreed that the Archons were forbidden to invade our world in force so long as there is a viable culture here. That's why the Archons have worked so hard to bring disruption and chaos.

"To protect our world, the High King assigned the Irin to patrol the shadow realm and offer assistance, but within strict guidelines.

"That's where our world has been for the last twenty-thousand years.

"The human race has been reduced to a shadow of what it once was. As a result of the genetic damage inflicted, our life force is almost non-existent, our bodies get sick, grow old, and die very quickly. And we are continually tormented by the Archons.

"We've lived that way for so long, we've accepted it as normal. We've forgotten what we've lost. Only in our dreams do we see a picture of something more.

"But the Ancient Ones have long promised that

our race will one day be restored. That's a promise the Irin and the other races have clung to. They long to see our restoration. They remember what we once were.

"But we've now entered into a new era. The time for restoration has come. This is a time when everything we've lost will be restored. I was just the first.

"The High King told me that because I laid down my life to save my world, I was the first to experience the restoration.

"I did things today to rescue Lys, things not even an Irin could do. But I'm not a superhero or some kind of alien.

"I am a *human*. I'm *fully* human, a human as we were all meant to be. I am what the human race once was. My life force has been restored and my gifts activated.

"And I'm not unique. What you see in me is what the High King intends for all of us.

"Jamie, I told you on the beach that the time had come for the restoration of all we've lost. That's true for us in our relationship. But it is also true for our whole world.

"And that restoration *has* begun. I'm a prototype, but there are many more to follow. And once the final restoration begins, it will take place rapidly. This group, the Iona synaxis, will be first. Then the restoration will spread to other synaxis groups, and as the Archons are pushed back it will spread from them to the entire world.

"This was always part of the plan to defeat the

Archons. It's the only way the Archons can finally be overcome.

"But before any of that can happen, the chosen one must go to Hi-Ouranos and appear before the High King."

Roger was silent for a moment, then continued.

"But I have a warning for all of us.

"It had been agreed that I should keep my abilities secret until the time comes for the rest of the synaxis to be restored. But Lys's kidnapping forced my hand. I had no choice but to use my power to rescue her, and all of the Irin agreed with me on that.

"But that puts our whole world in great danger.

"The Archons know that when the restoration takes place, it will mean they've lost everything. They can no longer enslave us. They can no longer torture and torment us. They will never take our world for their own. They will be driven back to their own burned-out world and their evil influence removed from the Earth-realm.

"When I rescued Lys this morning, the Archons saw undeniable proof that restoration has taken place in at least one person. I'm sure they realize that the restoration of the rest of humanity will follow quickly.

"Knowing that the restoration has begun may drive the Archons to make a desperate move in an attempt to destroy all of us, before the final restoration can occur."

Marissa had been listening intently, drinking in

everything. But when Roger described a desperate move to destroy the human race, an icy chill traveled down her spine and her breath caught in her throat.

Looking around at the other members of the group, she spoke for the first time, "That desperate move may be closer than you think."

Chapter Twelve:
Marissa's Revelation

IONA HOUSE – THE ISLAND OF IONA

Marissa looked around at the members of the group. "I don't know if this is what Roger was talking about, but the Archons already have something big planned. The sheikh's palace has been buzzing about it for days. They have a plan they think will cause worldwide chaos, and it's all supposed to happen within the next few weeks.

"Their plan is to blow 27 airliners out of the sky at the same time. I don't know how they picked the number 27, but they say Kareina calculated it's the number that will produce the maximum effect. They say Kareina is providing them with a new kind of explosive that will pass through any kind of airport screening.

"As a result of that attack, air travel will cease permanently in every nation. Economies will collapse. The Archons see it rolling across nation after nation, like dominos. They believe it will lead to the total collapse of human civilization."

"Marissa, are you certain of this?"

"That was the sheikh's deal for Lys. I heard the guards talking about it when they brought Lys in. In exchange for Lys, the sheikh agreed to do something unprecedented. He will coordinate the actions of every major terror group on earth in one vast, devastating attack. They're calling it the Worldwide Day of Rage. I don't know the exact date, but it's sometime in the next few weeks."

The room fell silent.

"After four airliners were destroyed on 9/11," Michael said pensively, "air travel fell by more than thirty percent worldwide. It took years to recover. The only thing that saved the industry was a clever bit of theater called airport security. The TSA imposed ridiculous limitations that greatly inconvenienced innocent travelers, but the overall effect was that people felt safe to fly again. The reasoning was that if the TSA confiscated little Johnny's Boy Scout knife and grandma's knitting needles, the skies must certainly be safe from terrorists.

"But this would be a whole different scenario. Twenty-seven airliners blown out of the sky with an explosive the TSA couldn't detect would mean that no one is safe to fly. Ever. An attack of this magnitude could bring a permanent halt to air travel."

"That would definitely produce a lot of disruption," said Holmes. "But would it really cause civilization to collapse?"

"I believe it could," Michael answered. "The airline industry represents about three trillion dollars of the world's economy and employs close to 60 million people. Imagine 60 million people out of work, overnight. That's not counting the dozens of industries like hotels and resorts that rely on air travelers for their business. Add to that the fact that every major corporation now depends on air travel for their sales and customer service. So every corporation in the world takes a huge hit.

"And those 60 million newly unemployed people can no longer afford to build new homes or buy cars. So other industries are affected.

"A big part of our problem is that we no longer have alternative infrastructure," Michael added. "Before air travel became popular, we had an extensive rail passenger system and huge fleets of ships that ferried passengers across the oceans. But those no longer exist. It would take years to replace them.

"This isn't something that will produce rioting in the streets overnight, but the world's economy is very fragile. Over the course of several months, as industry after industry goes bankrupt, this truly could bring worldwide chaos."

"And if it doesn't put us completely over the edge," Holmes concluded, "I'm sure the Archons have something else in the works to take us the rest of the way."

Erin looked at Holmes. "I know we've exposed terror plots in the past, and thwarted a good number. Is there any we can prevent this?"

"I'm sure we'll get warnings about a number of these attacks," Holmes answered. "The second-sight gift seems to be strengthening. Almost every synaxis has at least one person with the second-sight gift, and many of them are becoming quite adept.

"But I don't think we can catch all of them. We're just not that strong yet. We might catch a third, maybe even half. We'll forward to the authorities all the information we get, but even if we can alert them to half the attacks, that still leaves at least thirteen airliners blown out of the sky in a single day. It will still cause worldwide chaos."

"What can we do?" asked Erin.

"What about Jamie's network," Patrick interjected. "We used it to find Lys. Would it work for this?

"What if we alerted every synaxis on earth and asked them to meet in an emergency synaxis to focus on airliner attacks."

"It's worth a try," Holmes agreed.

Erin looked from Holmes to Jamie. "Let's do it."

Jamie was already flipping her laptop open. "I'm on it. Within the next twelve to sixteen hours we should have heard back from most of the groups. I'll let you know what comes in.

The results poured in. With her wedding now just three days away, Jamie put her wedding preparations on temporary hold and spent the next morning collating the data.

Around 11 AM, Derek Holmes stopped by to see the results.

Seeing Holmes, Jamie held up a sheaf of papers. "We now have enough information to stop 26 of the attacks. I'm really impressed at the feedback we've received. The date is confirmed as fourteen days from now. We have departure cities and either times or flight numbers, along with the name of the passenger who'll be carrying the bomb."

"That leaves just one flight we just don't have actionable information on. I believe it will fly out of Frankfurt, Germany, but we just don't have enough detail. They're not going to shut down the whole Frankfurt airport based on the kind of information we have."

"Well done, Jamie. This should still be enough to stave off disaster," Holmes said. "I hate it that we can't get them all, but one aircraft destroyed is not going to set off worldwide chaos."

He started to dial his phone, then paused. "What time is it now in Virginia?"

Without needing to look it up, Jamie answered, "about six-thirty in the morning."

"I better wait a few hours. Stan doesn't like *anyone* to disturb his beauty sleep!

"Why don't we break for lunch?"

Coming back from lunch, Holmes was about to dial the phone when Jamie checked her laptop one more time.

"Wait, Holmes. Here's one more report. It just came in.

"It's from a little Inuit village on an island off the northwest coast of Alaska. The place is called Kivalina. They apologize for the delay. The men were all out hunting caribou on the tundra when our message came in. It took them a while to call the synaxis together."

"I remember that group," Holmes smiled. "It was one of the very first. Piper and I went there to help set up the synaxis. It's a tiny place. The whole village was probably less than 400 people. We flew there in a little six-seat puddle-jumper that also delivered the mail. It landed on a gravel runway on the edge of the Arctic Ocean. It was about as remote a place as you could imagine, but the people were incredible. If I remember correctly, in addition to other gifts, their synaxis began with at least four people who had a second-sight gift. Some of them were already pretty skilled.

"What kind of information did they get for us?"

As Jamie skimmed the report, her mouth dropped open in unbelief.

"This is it, Holmes! What they saw was the Frankfurt attack. They gave us the flight number, the seat assignment, the name. It's all here!

"We've got all twenty-seven!"

Stanley F. Allen was the associate deputy director of the CIA's Counterterrorism center with a spacious office on the sixth floor of the CIA headquarters building in Langley, Virginia. The CIA's Counterterrorism Center had been established in 1986 to facilitate the sharing of information and to improve response times to terrorist threats. It had proven to be one of the most effective tools for combating the worldwide menace of terrorism.

The call came in on his personal cell phone. Stanley answered it on the third ring, having first checked the caller ID.

"Hey, Stanley, how's my favorite spook?"

"Derek Holmes!" Stan laughed in response.

"My favorite shrink!"

Stan and Derek had been friends since college, where they'd both been defensive linemen for the University of Texas' Longhorns. They'd done their best to stay in touch over the years, often doing a round of golf when Stanley was in town visiting family.

"Got any more hot leads for me?"

"Stan, my man, I've got a lead like you wouldn't believe. I just received hard intel on a plot to take down 27 commercial aircraft in a single day. The plan is designed to shut down air travel on a worldwide scale. I can give you flight times, flight numbers, locations, and the names of the suicide bombers. As an added bonus, I can also give you the name and location of the mastermind behind the attacks.

There was silence on the line for a moment, then Stan spoke, "Derek, I have to ask again... where are you getting this stuff? I mean, it's been what? ...fifteen times in the last few months?"

"Have I ever been wrong?"

"No, you've nailed it every time. Lives have been saved."

Stan paused again, getting very serious. "But people are starting to talk, my friend. How is a former psychologist in Dallas, Texas getting impossibly high-level intel on every major terrorist organization in earth?"

"Sorry pal, I can't reveal my sources. As they say in your business, if I told you I'd have to kill you.

"But," Holmes said, sobering quickly, "this one

is serious, Stan. It goes way beyond anything I've ever given you. There's too much data to tell you over the phone, so I sent the file to your personal email address. Let me know if it doesn't show up."

"I see it in my in-box right now. I'll take a look."

"Stanley, what you see before you may be the most important email ever sent."

Chapter Thirteen: Wedding Day

THE ISLAND OF IONA

This is the day I've dreamt of all my life!

Lys stood side-by-side with Jamie Thatcher, gazing across the beautiful white-sand beach of *Port Ban*. Their friends were already gathering. The day had been warm and clear, and the sun now hung low in a cloudless sky. Both Lys and Jamie were resplendent in white wedding gowns.

Lys had begun the day sharing a leisurely breakfast with Roger, together with her mom and dad, catching up on old times. The family had always been close, and she had truly missed spending time with her folks since she'd moved to Scotland, especially on holidays. Her parents had only met Patrick a few times, so they had many questions, and of course they were curious about the synaxis.

For lunch, Lys met with Patrick and his parents. They were both anxious to find out more about Lys, but his dad was also excited to show them photos of his newly acquired home in Northern Ireland. It was the first time Lys had met Patrick's folks and she decided she really liked them.

The afternoon had been a flurry of activity. A hairdresser had driven over from Oban to do both Lys and Jamie's hair. The seamstress had also come, to make any final adjustments on the gowns.

Then, as evening approached, Erin had driven Lys and Jamie to the beach, to spend a few minutes together before the festivities began. This was their day, and it seemed impossible that it was real.

Standing at the edge of the beach in their wedding gowns, Lys gazed at Jamie for a long moment, fighting back tears. "Jamie, you look so beautiful. I'm so happy things finally worked out between you and Roger. Even when I was a kid and flew up to visit Roger in Colorado, I was so impressed with you. I always hoped you'd be my sister-in-law."

"You don't know how thankful I am to be getting you for *my* sister-in-law, Lys! After my folks died, the only family I had left was my sister. We'd always been close, and having just each other seemed to draw us even closer. Even though we lived in different cities, we made a point of sharing our lives. Every Saturday night Becky and I would connect on Skype, pour a glass of wine, and spend time catching up on our week.

"But after Becky was killed, I had nothing. I had no family, no one who cared. I felt I was all alone in the world.

"But now that's all changed. First of all, I have Roger, which is nothing short of a miracle, and the whole synaxis seems more and more like a family. But beyond all of that, Lys, when I'm with you I feel like I have a sister again."

"I'm so glad." Lys said, embracing Jamie warmly, "and I'll have a glass of wine with you any time you want."

Lys watched friends making final adjustments on the wedding canopy and adding fuel to the torches.

Jamie spoke again, "This whole thing seems like a dream come true. I have to keep pinching myself to be sure it's not a dream."

"I know what you mean. I've been thinking about that all day.

"Four mornings ago, I woke up naked on the concrete floor of the sheikh's torture chamber. I felt like my life was over. But today I'm back on Iona with the people I love, and getting married to my best friend in the world."

The sun was almost to the horizon. It was almost time for the ceremony to begin.

A beach wedding wasn't exactly what Lys had always envisioned. As a little girl she'd imagined a big church wedding, very formal, with lots of attendants. This was definitely not that, but she found she actually liked it better.

Doing a beach wedding had required some compromises. She'd loved the idea of wearing heels, but the seamstress who did her gown strongly recommended flat sandals. "They're much more practical on the beach. On a beach, the heels won't make you any taller. They'll just sink into the sand and make it hard to walk." Lys had finally yielded to her logic.

The other issue had been the veil. The seamstress had recommended against one. "They tend to blow around a lot and get in the way during an outdoor wedding."

But since Lys knew *Port Ban* was pretty much

sheltered from the wind, she decided to go for a veil anyhow. *It might blow around a little,* she reasoned, *but it could actually look beautiful, billowing gracefully in the breeze.*

Fortunately, Lys and Jamie had similar tastes. Both wanted a romantic, simple, short ceremony.

Being a beach wedding, neither saw the need for many decorations. The beautiful beach was decoration enough.

A simple wooden framework had been erected in the center of the beach, four upright posts joined at the top with a canopy, decorated with white flowers and greenery.

Marty Shapiro, a friend from the first synaxis who had come for the ceremony, took one look and beamed, "You've got a *chupah!* A Jewish wedding canopy!"

They'd decided against setting up chairs, since they were determined to keep the ceremony short. Instead, they'd asked the guests to gather around close, once the brides and grooms were together under the canopy. Lys and Jamie both thought it would make the occasion more intimate.

Since they both had the same circle of friends, Jamie and Lys had decided to share bridesmaids and groomsmen. Half were human, and half Irin.

Bridesmaids included Eliel, Rand, Reetha, and Erin.

Groomsmen included Araton and Khalil, along with Marty Shapiro and Ron Lewis from the original synaxis.

Holmes and Piper agreed to serve as the best

man and matron of honor for both couples.

Choreographing a double wedding on the beach had taken some thought, but Lys was pleased with the result.

As the sun dipped below the horizon, more of their friends gathered. Cars arrived with the rest of the wedding party. Torches were lit.

When the time came for the ceremony to begin, the grooms entered and stood on opposite sides of the minister under the wooden framework.

Then the bridesmaids and groomsmen came in from opposite directions and formed a circle around the canopy.

Catherine Campbell sang a beautiful Gaelic love song, then Angus and Malcolm began playing "Highland Cathedral" on the bagpipe and highland flute.

That meant it was her turn. Lys's dad offered her his arm, and she took it, leaning over to give him a quick peck on the cheek. "I love you, Daddy. Thank you so much for everything you've done for me."

They began a slow walk toward the canopy. As Lys held her father's arm, walking from the south, she knew Michael was escorting Jamie from the north.

It seemed like the longest walk of her life. As she glanced around at all the friends gathered for the occasion, tears welled in her eyes.

She loved the feel of the sand crunching under her feet. *So glad I didn't wear heels!*

Her eyes were now fixed on Patrick. As always, he looked at least a week overdue for a haircut, but he was well-built with a warm smile. He was also her best friend. She realized again how much she truly did love him.

As they came under the canopy, Lys's dad gave her a kiss, then took her hand and placed it in Patrick's. Despite the archaic symbolism, both Jamie and Lys liked the idea of being "given in marriage."

When the music finished, the old minister, speaking in a thick Scottish brogue, began, "Dearly beloved, we are gathered here today in the sight of God and this company to join these two couples in the bonds of holy matrimony..."

After a brief sermon, the minister, who was clearly stretched beyond his comfort zone but performing like a trooper, first addressed Lys and Patrick, and led them in their vows.

He then turned to Roger and Jamie and led them in theirs.

Then, turning from one couple to another, he made a common pronouncement, "I now declare you to be husband and wife!"

As both couples kissed, Rand and Eliel unfurled their wings, rose from the ground, and with bodies glowing brilliantly, began to circle the *chupah*. Suddenly they were joined in the sky by hundreds of glowing Irin, lighting up the night sky as they circled the beach, flying with ever increasing speed, they danced an intricate dance in the sky over *Port Ban*.

It was a dance never before seen on earth. Streams of glowing Irin flew in braided patterns around the beach, then rose in graceful pirouettes, twirling rapidly with arms extended.

Angling their wings to catch the currents that

flow between the dimensions, they began executing a series of graceful twirls and loops, rising higher, all the while encircling the beach. The whole company soared high above the beach, then, extending their wings, made a long, triumphant spiral down to circle just above the *chupah* again.

And then they began to sing, a song no human had ever heard. It was beautiful as it rose to crescendo after crescendo. Though none of the humans understood the words, the song painted pictures in their minds. Pictures of beauty unexcelled. Love, joy, and unending peace. The passion of a lover's embrace. The tenderness of a mother with a newborn baby. On and on they sang as tears of joy flowed freely down Lys's face.

As the angel dance concluded, wild applause went up from the assembled crowd. Then Araton handed Roger a sword, which instantly began to scintillate with golden light. Roger faced toward the northeast, lifted the sword over his head, and brought it down in a swift stroke. With a sound like the rumble of distant thunder, a rift opened.

"Now everyone," Araton boomed joyfully as he stepped toward the rift. "Follow me to the reception!"

A large fire had been kindled on the beach behind Iona House, surrounded by tables laden with food and drink. The deck of Iona House had been transformed into a dance floor.

After a lot of mingling and small talk, the time came for Lys to dance with her father. He held her in a paternal embrace as they glided around the dance floor. "Someday you and I are going to have a long talk," he whispered. "I don't understand half of what just happened, and I'd love to know more. For right now, I just know that my daughter and my son both seem happier than I've ever seen them. What more can a father ask?"

The honeymoon accommodations had been arranged by the Irin and were promised to be literally out of this world. At the close of the festivities, the wedding party walked down the road, and the two couples climbed the gentle slope to *cnoc nan carnan*. The members of the Iona synaxis gathered around them.

The portal, of course, was already open. The synaxis met weekly on *cnoc nan carnan* to strengthen and maintain the tenuous wormhole that linked the worlds. Looking up, they could see the faint outline of a tunnel that penetrated into the depths of the sky.

They were not here this time to open a portal, but to traverse one. Four humans were about to travel through the wormhole to another world. Patrick and Lys stood on one side of the portal, while Jamie and Roger stood on the other. The Irin circled overhead.

Lys began to sing. The song rose from deep within her and flowed out, syllable after syllable. The song increased in volume. It had rhythm and meter, and the melody grew more complex.

Suddenly, through the tunnel, came a shaft of brilliant light. The light was more than white. It was a shimmering rainbow of blinding radiance, brighter than the brightest day. The light from the heavens enveloped the four, and they were gone.

Chapter Fourteen:
The Final Contingency

THE RUINS OF AN ANCIENT ARCHON
SPACEPORT – IN THE DESERT NEAR ABADON

The tunnel was long, narrow, and obviously hastily dug, lit only by a dull red glow emanating from the rocks themselves. Stacked beside the entrance, the bodies of several slaves who had literally been worked to death were slowly mummifying in the intense, dry heat of Hades.

Kareina traversed the crude tunnel, which ran for several hundred yards. The descent was steep in places, and in other places there were indications that cave-ins had taken place during the excavation. Emerging finally from the tunnel, Kareina stopped, awestruck by the sight of the huge gallery it had led her to.

Kareina had seen the place before, more than 20,000 years ago. It was part of the main spaceport of Abadon—a huge underground hangar that once housed the scores of ships that brought the wealth of the solar system to the city.

Before the collapse of Archon civilization at the end of the great wars, the Archons had been a spacefaring race, with bases on the moon and Mars, and mining operations in the asteroid belt. They had even constructed a portal among the asteroids, allowing them to trade their riches with other realms.

The spaceport was now in ruins. In the last battles of the great wars, the roof of the hangar had collapsed, burying most of the ships under tons of debris and heavily damaging the rest. Shifting sands had long since enshrouded the place. No visible trace of the spaceport was left on the surface.

By the end of the great wars, the technology for space travel had been lost. The Archon scientists and engineers had all been killed in the devastating attacks on the Archon cities. It was estimated that more than 90% of the total Archon population had been lost. Though the normal Archon lifespan ran to tens of thousands of years, it was now rare to find someone who remembered the world before the wars. Kareina was one of the few.

The spaceport had been buried for twenty-thousand years, forgotten by almost everyone. But Kareina remembered. When the High Counsel approved her latest plan, she'd put gangs of slaves to work, operating in shifts twenty-four hours a day, for two months. A passage to the hangar had finally been opened.

Kareina drew a deep breath. She was feeling her age. Though her hatred for the human race had not diminished, she had grown weary of the battle. In recent years, she had suffered two humiliating defeats at the hands of the synaxis, and had a nagging feeling that the present plan was not going well at all.

First, there had been the disturbing figures showing that the synaxis groups were multiplying faster than she had anticipated. They were already interfering significantly with her plans. Some of her most carefully calculated attacks had been thwarted. If the present plan failed, there could be only one remaining backup.

And now news had come that a restored human had apparently breached their highest level of security to rescue Lys Johnston. If the restoration of humanity had already begun, they had very little time. She had to be certain everything was in place for the final contingency. And that demanded that the spaceport be reopened.

Archon engineers were still far from the level of expertise obtained by their ancestors, but they were diligently working to recapture the ancient knowledge. Kareina had arranged to meet the head engineer in the ruined hangar.

The place was depressing. As she walked through dusty piles of debris, seeing the hulks of ancient spacecraft that lay crushed and demolished, her hatred of the human race burned with even greater intensity. She remembered proud ships rising gloriously from their docking cradles, headed outward to the furthest reaches of the solar system.

Other ships were arriving, laden with treasure from the mines of Mars and the asteroid belt. The ground crews hurried to keep everything running smoothly, loading and unloading, with timetables accurate to less than a minute, a tribute to the efficiency of Archon civilization.

But that had all been lost. When the Archon forces refused to abandon their efforts to conquer the

Earth-realm, the Ancient Ones had declared total war against the realm of Hades. Fighters had come from every inhabited realm. City after city was destroyed, but the Archons did not surrender easily.

In the end, however, they had no choice. The Archon race was decimated, and Archon civilization destroyed. And at the root of it all was the hated human race, and their stubborn resistance to Archon rule.

For twenty-thousand years now the Archons had worked to overcome the humans, but had been defeated at every hand. But if this last plan worked, the long delayed victory would finally be theirs.

At the far end of the hangar, Kareina found the chief engineer, pulling clumps of wire from the ruins of a smashed instrument panel. The engineer was young, far younger than she was. To him, the lost Archon civilization was a study in ancient history. The spaceport merely an archaeological site, a matter of curiosity. But he was the best mind the Archons had.

After a brief greeting, the engineer gestured out across the jumble of ruined spacecraft.

"There are no undamaged ships," he explained. "But it may be possible to salvage parts from several of the least damaged ones to reconstruct a ship that will fly."

Pointing to a small cargo hauler that appeared to be relatively undamaged, he said, "This ship is probably our best option. If I can find the right parts, it could be ready to fly in a matter of weeks."

"What about pilots? Do we have anyone who

can fly a ship once we have it?"

"That may be harder. So far as I know, all of our pilots were killed in the great wars. I'm still searching the database, but it doesn't look hopeful. It may be possible to train someone, but it will take time."

"Time is what we do *not* have," Kareina growled. "We need a ship and a pilot. One ship. One pilot."

"I'll do my best, but I can't give you any guarantees."

"Find them," Kariena repeated. "One ship and one pilot.

"That's all I need. But I *must* have them!"

Chapter Fifteen: Rashid's Story

FRANKFURT AM MAIN AIRPORT – FRANKFURT, GERMANY

The deep rumble of a 767 taking off from the *Frankfurt am Main* airport filled the cheap hotel room, vibrating the pictures on the walls and rattling the glass on the bathroom counter.

Rashid cringed. The jet's roar reminded him of the thunder of Soviet helicopters passing low over his house as a child.

He lay awake, staring at the ceiling. This would be his last night on earth. Tomorrow he would enter paradise, welcomed by a throng of 72 beautiful virgins.

The Soviet War in Afghanistan had been a ten-year long disaster. The Soviets claimed to be defending the Marxist government of Afghanistan against the *mujahidin* resistance. Their initial deployment began on December 24, 1979 under Soviet leader Leonid Brezhnev and was soon hopelessly mired.

In 1986, with the war heading into its seventh year, and no closer to victory, the Soviets invented a hellish strategy.

They developed a series of mines designed to

look like toys, dolls, watches, and ball-point pens. Filled with liquid explosives, they were intended to attract the curiosity of children, and explode when picked up.   The most widely used was dubbed the butterfly bomb.   Officially known as the PFM-1 scatterable pressure-sensitive blast mine, it was shaped like a green plastic butterfly.

"Butterfly bombs" consisted of two plastic petals around an explosive charge, dropped from helicopters to a gentle landing on the ground.

Soviet helicopters scattered more than eight million of these anti-personnel mines around Afghan villages, all along the the Misamsha-Khost border.   They armed upon impact, waiting for someone to step on one or pick it up.

The Soviet strategy was designed to induce terror, demoralizing the resistance fighters and bringing a quick surrender. It had the opposite effect.

It filled the entire region with burning hatred for all infidel outsiders.

Rashid's father, Pazhman Harkani, had never been an overly religious man, though he faithfully said his daily prayers. He was a simple man who loved his home and loved his family. The furtherest he had ever traveled from his ancestral home was the bazaar at Angoor Adda, a few kilometers to the east, near the Pakistani border.

When Pazhman wasn't tending his apple orchard, he loved to sit on the bench in front of his mud-brick hut and gaze eastward at the mountains. To the east, an expanse of forested ridges rose to 9,500 feet, marking the border with Pakistan. Pazhman often wondered what was on the other side of the mountains, but never had enough curiosity to try to find out. He was content with his own world.

Then the Soviets came.

The joy of Pazhman's life was his little daughter Mitra. She was a chubby five-year old, with a bubbly personality and a love of life. Watching Mitra play filled him with happiness.

It had been a sunny morning and Pazhman was sitting on the wooden bench by the door of his house as Mitra played in the apple orchard.

"Papa!" she squealed in delight, "Look what I've found!" Pazhman looked up to see Mitra running toward him, her chubby arms holding what appeared to be a large green-plastic butterfly.

Recognizing immediately what it was, he screamed, "No! Mitra! Put that down!"

But it was too late. With a brutal retort like the firing of a high-powered rifle, the butterfly mine exploded.

Both of Mitra's hands were instantly blown off, along with half of her face and a good part of her chest, but she was still conscious, screaming in agony.

Knowing that there was no chance that she could live, Pazhman ran to her, took her gently in his arms and rocked her as the life drained from her broken little body. It took her twenty minutes to die.

Rashid's mother Khatira died a few months later from a broken heart. Pazhman never recovered. A darkness came over him. It was almost visible at times. He had erratic mood swings, but mostly he was filled with rage.

He talked about nothing but his hatred of the infidels. Two months later he joined the *mujahidin*.

He sent Rashid to the madras, the local religious school, and beat him if he didn't do his lessons. Rashid became a *Talib*, a religious student trained in the ways of militant Islam, and he learned to hate as well.

Rashid took his seat, row 23, seat A, by the window as he had requested. He checked the space between the arm rest and the outer wall of the plane. There would be plenty of room to insert the booby-trapped laptop, when the time came. The seat had been carefully chosen, so that a violent rupture in the outer wall of the aircraft would also take out vital control circuits.

Rashid fiddled with the seat controls. *Look bored. Blend in*, he told himself.

He watched the infidels streaming down the aisles, like cattle to the slaughterhouse. Many stopped and tried to jam overly large bags into the cramped overhead compartments. They were being so careful, so protective of their belongings. They didn't realize they would never see those things again.

As the flow of passengers down the aisle dwindled, Rashid glanced around the cabin. The seat next to him was still vacant. That meant a more comfortable flight. A number of other seats were unoccupied, more than he'd expected. He noted that both of the seats behind him were unoccupied also. But there were still enough passengers to make a powerful statement. Just across the aisle from him a mother, father, and little girl, almost Mitra's age, had just taken their seats. They looked so happy and carefree. But this day they would die. His rage against the infidels would be fully displayed today.

The flight attendant came down the aisle, closing the overhead compartments. She smiled at him as she went past. She was a slender blonde in her mid-thirties. He smiled back and nodded. *You will die also!*

The doors closed and the plane was pushed back from the gate. A pre-recorded safety film began playing on the screen in front of him.

Suddenly, the safety presentation was interrupted by a voice from the cockpit. "This is Captain Abrams. Folks, I've got bad news and good news. The bad news is, we've discovered a mechanical problem. The good news is that we have the part in stock and mechanics are standing by. It should take less than an hour to fix. We'll be returning to the gate, but I ask that you please remain in your seats. I apologize for the delay, but we should be able to make up most of the lost time in our flight across the pond, so those of you with connecting flights should not be greatly affected."

Rashid leaned back in his seat as plane returned to the gate and the door was opened. The small delay would affect nothing.

Two men in mechanics uniforms carrying tool kits boarded the plane and walked toward the back of the cabin.

Just as they passed his seat, a third mechanic

entered, walking more slowly.

The third mechanic paused, and was looking directly at him. Rashid sensed in his gut that something was wrong. He was about to reach for the laptop case under the seat in front of him, when strong hands grasped his head from behind and plunged a hypodermic needle into his neck. The third mechanic was already on him, grabbing his hands and holding them tightly as the drug took effect, preventing him from detonating the bomb.

Chapter Sixteen: Transition

THE SHEIK'S PALACE – DEEP IN THE ARABIAN DESERT

The whirlwind formed in the ring of standing stones — a dark storm of swirling sand-wind.

Within minutes, the spectral form of the desert demon appeared, and rapidly passed through the Bedouin camp to enter the fortress of *Qasr-Al-Djinn*.

A guard met Kareina at the elevator door.

"Tell the sheikh I must speak to him immediately."

The sheikh entered the room in less than five minutes, clearly apprehensive. He'd been awaiting a report on the terror attacks, but so far there was nothing in the news.

"How is the Day of Rage progressing?" He asked tentatively.

"The operation has failed!" Kareina growled, glaring at him with eyes that burned with hellish fire. "All 27 bombers were caught before takeoff."

"But I did everything you asked!"

"It makes no difference. The operation is over. With the worldwide synaxis threat growing in strength daily, terrorism will no longer serve our purposes."

"We have no further use for you, but I must warn you, the Americans now know where you are.

A joint US-Jordanian task force will be here within hours to take you captive.

A look of horror came across the sheikh's twisted face.

"But what can I do?" He whined. "I have nowhere to go!" Then a thought formed in his demented mind. "Take me with you!" he pleaded, "Take me to Hades. I'll do anything you want."

Kareina paused a moment, toying with the idea.

"You do have useful skills," she said thoughtfully. "You are, in fact, more adept in torturing humans than any Archon I know."

Her lips tightened in a sinister grin. "We could assign you to work in one of the lower levels of the arena. That's where the most agonizing torments take place… it could be very entertaining."

She paused a moment longer, then made her decision. "Very well. Come with me."

"Please give me a few minutes to gather some things."

"You have five minutes, no longer."

The sheikh ran to his harem one more time. Its current occupant was a Bedouin slave girl, barely thirteen years old. Her naked, emaciated body was badly bruised and lay motionless in a pool of congealed blood.

The sheikh bent down to look at her one last time, but saw that she was already dead.

He picked up a few items from his office and bed chamber then met Kareina at the elevator.

"Hold your position!" he barked at the guards

as the elevator doors began to slide shut. "Our enemies are coming!"

The men in the Bedouin encampment looked on in amazement as they saw the sheikh leaving the fortress with Kareina. He walked with the *djinn* to the circle of stones, and both disappeared in a whirlwind of swirling sand.

Arriving in the Great Portal of Abadon, the sheikh gazed around at his new world. A barren wasteland stretched as far as he could see. Clouds of yellow, sulfurous dust scudded across the lifeless plain. The place was oppressively hot.

Not so different from home really, though the pervasive smell of Sulphur will take some getting used to.

Far to the right rose jagged skeletons of dark, twisted steel — the remains of the original city of Abadon. Immediately behind him he saw a mountain range. Volcanos were erupting in the distance. On a cliff face, just 300 feet away, yawned the entrance of an immense cavern.

"Follow me," Kareina said as she passed from the circle of standing stones and walked briskly toward the cave. "I'll take you to Lucifer, the arena master. He'll show you your new responsibilities and assign your new accommodations. You won't find your lodgings here to be as luxurious as your palace, but I assure you, for Hades they will be quite pleasant... And I'm certain that you *will* enjoy your work."

As they strode down the main corridor of the city, Kareina tapped a code into her communicator.

The chief engineer answered almost immediately.

"Do we have a ship?"

"Yes, Kareina, I was able to scrounge the parts for that old cargo hauler I showed you. We just completed the final testing. I'm certifying that it's ready to fly."

"What about a pilot?"

"We were very fortunate. One pilot has survived. She doesn't have a great deal of experience, but she appears to be familiar with the controls. I believe she can do what we need."

"One ship and one pilot," Kareina repeated again. "That's all we need. With that we will prevail.

"Put the final contingency plan into operation. The time has come for the destruction of the human race."

PART THREE: THE COMET

Chapter Seventeen: Belphegor

FIVE MONTHS LATER – IN ORBIT AROUND THE PLANET JUPITER.

The comet nucleus was almost a mile across — millions of tons of stone and ice slowly spinning in the darkness of space.

Approaching the immense floating mountain, Belphegor eased her thrusters, carefully adjusting the ship's trajectory.

It would be a tricky maneuver. The comet was shaped like a lopsided dumbbell, with many scars and craters. The main body looked like a lumpy, deformed egg, but another chunk of rock and ice, a thousand feet in diameter, clung precariously to it, connected by a slender neck less than fifty feet across. To make matters worse, the whole surface of the comet was shrouded in haze, as the distant sun slowly sublimated the comet's volatile compounds.

Belphegor gripped the controls more firmly, her eyes fixed unwaveringly on the computer screen before her.

Belphegor had the appearance of an ancient gargoyle, with a broad, deeply ridged forehead, leathery skin, and stubby, goat-like horns; but her bulging green reptilian eyes burned with cruel intelligence. Firing the thrusters intermittently to reduce her speed, her thickly muscled jaws spread wide revealing a double row of razor-sharp fangs.

The computer had pinpointed the optimal landing site and the display showed her altitude, ticking off the markers as she approached touchdown.

6... 5... 4... 3... One more touch on the thrusters and the old cargo hauler eased to a landing on the comet's surface. The moment of impact was barely discernable.

Belphegor breathed a sigh of relief. She had traveled four months out from Hades, then traversed the ancient portal in the asteroid belt to enter Earth-realm space. Her job was now nearly complete.

Though the journey had been long and lonely, it felt good to be piloting a ship again. Kareina had chosen Belphegor because twenty-thousand years earlier, she had once piloted a craft into space. As near as Kareina could determine, Belphegor was the only Archon still living who had actually handled the controls of a spacecraft.

Belphegor had known from the start that this was a suicide mission. The journey outward, and the fuel she would expend to accomplish her task, would tax the small ship's resources to its limits. There could be no return home. The life-support system was already faltering. She would be dead long before the ship reached its destination.

She double-checked her calculations one last time. In less than three hours it would be time to fire the ship's powerful main engines. That would begin the process of easing the comet into its new trajectory.

Chapter Eighteen: The Anniversary

IONA HOUSE - ONE YEAR AFTER THE DOUBLE WEDDING

"Happy anniversary!" Marissa beamed as she entered the main dining room of Iona House to find Patrick and Lys already seated, eating breakfast.

"Thank you," Lys smiled. "I can't believe it's been one year today. Come and join us!"

"Let me get some wake-up juice and I'll be right there."

Marissa had left Iona shortly after the wedding to testify at a UN committee on the incident at Erba Abdol. She'd then returned to Iraq to finish out her commitment with the World Health Organization. With her commitment fulfilled, Marissa had returned to Iona a few days ago to join the Synaxis.

"It's good to have you back," Patrick said as Marissa took her seat across from them.

"It's good to be back!" Marissa answered. "Understanding the Archons gave me a whole new perspective on what's happening in Iraq. I loved being able to help the people there, but just giving medical aid is never going to win the battle. I couldn't wait to get back here, to be part of the real fight."

Lys glanced at Marissa and their eyes met.

Both understood the bond between them. Just as her time in Hades had created an unbreakable tie with Jamie, so her time in the sheikh's torture chamber had formed an unspoken bond between her and Marissa.

"I know what you mean," Lys agreed. "Once you see the true nature of the evil, you want to fight it with everything that's in you."

"So what have you and Patrick been doing for the past year?"

"We've spent close to half of our time traveling," Patrick said. "Erin sends us out to help establish and strengthen the new synaxis groups popping up all over the place. When we're not traveling, we come back here to Iona House and help maintain the portal."

"This is a great place to come back to." Marissa said, taking a sip of her coffee, and glancing around the room. "I love being here."

Erin Fletcher, who led the local synaxis, had set up Iona House as a private bed and breakfast for synaxis members.

One of the highpoints of the day at Iona House was breakfast. The breakfasts tended to be social gatherings, with small groups clustered around the long wooden tables in the dining room. It was a time to visit, discuss the events of the day, and plan activities.

Because of their culinary skills, Erin had hired Catherine and Casey as in-house chefs, a job they both truly loved. The two always seemed to be trying to outdo themselves, whether it was with traditional

Scottish fare, or their own creative recipes.

Breakfast was provided daily for all synaxis members and their guests. For lunch and dinner, the synaxis members were on their own, though everyone enjoyed kitchen privileges. There were also frequent evening feasts and a nightly wine and cheese buffet.

Right after Casey took Marissa's breakfast order, Roger and Jamie entered the dining room.

"More newlyweds!" Marissa smiled broadly. "Come and join us!"

"Hi Marissa! It's good to see you! Let us get some coffee and we'll be right there," Roger replied.

On their way to the table, Roger and Jamie detoured by the sideboard. As always, the sideboard featured a lavish selection — several kinds of juices, yogurt, and fresh fruit. Toast was also available — white or wheat — cut diagonally, then slipped into a little rack to keep it crisp. Next to the toast was a large slab of butter, along with pots of orange marmalade and organic honey.

The sideboard also featured a variety of teas, along with coffee, available with skim milk, half and half, or Bailey's Irish Cream. Espresso and cappuccino could be ordered from the kitchen.

Roger and Jamie each picked up a container of yogurt, poured themselves some black coffee, and took seats next to Marissa, just across from Patrick and Lys.

"Roger and I were so glad to hear you've come back to Iona and joined the synaxis!" Jamie said as they took their seats.

"It's good to be here," Marissa said. "I just returned from Iraq last week.

"This is the first time I've seen the two of you since I've been back," she added. "Where have you been?"

"Erin sent us to visit some of the synaxis groups in England. It was a great trip. I can't believe how fast things are changing."

"How many groups are there now?"

"It's hard to say exactly," Jamie replied, taking a sip of her coffee. "New groups are popping up almost daily. In England alone there are over 300. Worldwide it's just over thirty-five hundred.

"And the change has been incredible. A lot of sections of the UK feel almost like Iona now. As synaxis members have begun to operate in their gifts, the Archons are being driven off. I read that crime is down 47% in Edinburgh, 56% in Manchester, and 32% in London. And the economy is booming."

"And it's not just crime," Roger added. "With the influence of the Archons on the wane and the shades almost extinct, divorce is down 60% and child abuse down 80%. To put it short, people are just happier now."

"So much of the human suffering we took for granted was a direct result of the evil Archon influence," Patrick agreed.

"Holmes tells me it's pretty a bad time for psychologists though," Roger laughed, "Their business is down 60%."

"And doctors too!" Jamie poked him in the arm, smiling playfully. "Word has gotten out that most synaxis groups have healers. More and more, people are tending to look up a nearby synaxis instead of going to a clinic. And when a healing takes place, it usually results in several new synaxis members!"

Just then, Casey came in from the kitchen, bringing Marissa's breakfast order. Seeing that Roger and Jamie had arrived, she brought them each a printed copy of the breakfast menu for the day.

"Welcome home!" she smiled. "What can I get you two for breakfast?"

"Everything looks so good, Casey," Jamie said as she scanned the menu. "I shouldn't eat too much for breakfast though. I've heard that you and Catherine are planning a big anniversary celebration feast for us this evening.

"I'll try something light. How about the avocado and poached egg on sourdough toast with roasted tomatoes?"

"Not me!" Roger beamed. "I'm famished. I'll have the full Scottish breakfast with the eggs over easy."

A full Scottish breakfast at Iona House consisted of half a tomato, broiled with cheddar cheese on top, a potato scone, link sausage, sautéed mushrooms, baked beans, and two free-range eggs.

As Casey finished taking their orders, Araton, Eliel, and Rand came in and joined them at the long table.

After assuring Casey that they'd already eaten, they poured themselves some coffee with Bailey's Irish Cream.

While they were waiting for their food, Patrick glanced at Eliel. "I've had a very disturbing dream the last few nights."

"What was it?"

"The dream begins the same way every night, but each night new details are added. I was in a place that looked like the descriptions I've heard of Hades.

"At the start of the dream, I was looking out across the crater of an extinct volcano. It was huge. It must have been a half-mile across. And it was filled with people. There must have been millions of them. Jammed in. Living in unbelievable filth and squalor. It looked like some kind of huge refugee camp.

"More humans were being added to the group almost continually. Several times an hour, groups of terrified new slaves were brought in by Archon guards and released into the crater.

"Overhead, were creatures I recognized as banshees, monstrous green-eyed nightmares, screeching and diving at the frightened humans."

"I remember that crater," Lys said. "When we were there it was used as a training ground for the Archon armies. They were preparing for an invasion of the Earth-realm. Since they are no longer preparing to invade us, it sounds like they've repurposed it."

A look of concern clouded Eliel's face. "That dream confirms what we've been sensing, Patrick. I believe what you saw was real. We've had a growing concern about this for several weeks now, and I've wanted to find an opportunity to talk with all of you about it.

"We know the Archons have not given up.

They always have a strategy. We just haven't been able to sense what it is.

"With all the good news in the last few months, there has been one thing that concerns us. Reports of missing persons are skyrocketing.

"I believe the Archons are using their remaining strength in the Earth-realm to accomplish just one thing. They're capturing massive numbers of humans and taking them back to Hades.

"Our fear is that the Archons are establishing a breeding colony of humans to maintain their slave supply when their access to our world has been finally cut off.

"I believe that's what you witnessed in your dreams."

Chapter Nineteen: Celebration Feast

IONA HOUSE – THE ISLAND OF IONA

The synaxis was always eager to find an excuse for a feast, and the one-year anniversary of a double wedding was too good an opportunity to pass up.

The Iona Synaxis had become like a close family, but the members were always on the move. They were constantly being sent out to help establish new synaxis groups somewhere in the world. So every gathering was like a family reunion, and Marissa's return had just added one more reason to celebrate.

The two newlywed couples stood together, looking out the French doors that faced the Sound of Iona. The sun was just setting and the distant mountains of Mull seemed to glow blood-red in the dying light.

A storm had blown in that morning and a cold rain had fallen most of the day. The sky had finally cleared, but a strong north wind still whipped up whitecaps on Iona Sound.

"It looks cold out there," Lys said

"It *is* cold." Patrick said, slipping his arm around her waist and pulling her close. "I'm thankful for the warmth of Iona House."

A big fire had been kindled in the fireplace of

the main living area, and several who had just arrived were clustered around it, warming up.

"I'm so thankful we had a nicer day than this last year!" Lys smiled, "A beach wedding on a day like this would not have been fun."

"We were fortunate," said Roger. "This is pretty late in the year on Iona, and storms are always a threat.

"Though they won't admit it, I still think the Irin had a hand in the weather that day."

"I agree." Jamie laughed. "I think the Irin are involved in a lot of things they don't admit. But I'm glad they are here."

Just then, the door opened and Holmes and Piper came in.

"Holmes and Piper!" Lys shouted with excitement. "It's so good to see you!"

"We wouldn't miss the big anniversary party! And besides, there's a rumor that Catherine and Casey are fixing an extraordinary feast."

Holmes and Piper had arrived in Scotland just that afternoon. It had been a long trip, but Lys and Patrick were both like extended family and they didn't want to miss their special day.

As Erin took their coats, Patrick took orders for their drinks.

"What will you have?"

"Something to warm us up," Holmes said. "How about coffee with Baileys?"

"Yes!" Piper said with a slight shiver as she stepped closer to the fire. "But make mine decaf with Baileys."

In a few moments, Patrick brought them their drinks. "Just what the doctor ordered!"

Patrick poured wine for himself and Lys, and they all found comfortable chairs.

"How's the Dallas synaxis going?" Lys asked as she sipped her wine.

"It's multiplying," Holmes said. "In fact, it's growing faster than we anticipated. As soon as we get more than twelve members in a group, we begin to think about dividing the group into two, so the groups are constantly changing."

Piper added. "We now have 32 synaxis groups in the Dallas area, and Archon activity is on the decline.

"Our main problem has been the American 'bigger-is-better' syndrome," Holmes laughed. "Some of the groups have tried to compete to be the 'biggest synaxis' in Dallas. The problem is, it doesn't work. Once you've got more than about 20 people, synaxis members tend to become spectators and aren't challenged to develop their gifts, which defeats the whole purpose."

"I hate to say it," Piper added, "but a lot of the new groups don't have the same 'family' feel that the original group had. I guess the main thing is that people are learning to use their gifts."

"And being set free from the Archons," Holmes added.

Fifteen minutes later, Catherine gave a loud whistle to call the group to attention, then announced that dinner was served.

Catherine and Casey had reprised one of their

favorite dishes, spicy venison stew.

Having savored the aroma for the last hour, everyone in the group was famished. They quickly found seats while Catherine and Casey brought out the food.

As they ate, Patrick glanced across the table at Michael. "Have you read the news about the comet?"

"No, Erin and I just got in from a whirlwind trip to Brazil. I haven't had time to check the news the last few days. Tell me about it."

"I first saw a note about it a week or two ago on an astronomy website. It's still pretty far off, but they've been able to compute its orbit more accurately now. It's supposed to come pretty close to the earth. It should be one of the best light-shows we've seen for centuries!"

A strange look clouded Michael's face. He was silent for a moment, then brightened. "Thanks Patrick, I'll check on that."

He paused a moment, took a sip of wine, then added, "I must tell you, Patrick, I have a strange feeling about that comet."

Comet Shoemaker-Levy impacting the planet Jupiter - 1994

Chapter Twenty: Wormwood

IONA HOUSE – THE ISLAND OF IONA

Erin woke at 6 AM the next morning to find Michael already seated in his recliner, iPad in hand, intently reading something, with a look of deep concern on his face.

"What is it Michael?"

"I've been reading about the new comet. They're saying it should give us a spectacular light show."

"A new comet?"

"Patrick told me about it last night. It's been in the news for several weeks but with all our travels I hadn't noticed it."

Erin shared Michael's causal interest in astronomy, and loved to check out the beautiful pictures from the Hubble telescope posted daily on NASA's "Astronomy Picture of the Day" website.

"Let me get some coffee and I'll join you." She said. "Can I fix you a cup?"

"Already working on one," he smiled, holding his cup up and then taking a gulp. "But thanks."

A moment later, Erin eased back on the recliner next to Michael's and took a sip of her coffee. "So tell me about this comet."

Michael scrolled back to the top of the page. "This site gives a good summary of what we know so far.

"The comet was discovered by Carl Davidson, an amateur astronomer from Taos, New Mexico, who whimsically named it Comet Wormwood after the mythical falling star of Biblical prophecy.

"At first, the comet was only mentioned in a small paragraph on a few astronomy websites, but as its trajectory was plotted more accurately, it has garnered more attention. Comet Wormwood is now expected to pass very close to the earth, offering a light-show unparalleled in centuries."

"When is it supposed to get here?"

"Its closest approach should be in about two months.

"...And this is interesting. It's one of the Jupiter-family comets."

Erin tilted her head to the left, which was her body language for *I don't understand what you're talking about.* "Jupiter family? I'm not familiar with that."

"Jupiter-family comets are unique because they orbit the planet Jupiter rather than orbiting the Sun. But their orbits are highly elliptical and very unstable. They don't orbit the planet in a neat little circle like a moon does. They travel out far from Jupiter, than come back around and swing in close, almost grazing the planet before heading back out into space. Sometimes they get too close, and actually hit Jupiter. At other times, something disturbs their orbit and they're thrown back out into space. Evidently, something diverted this one and sent it spinning toward us."

"So it sounds like Jupiter comets don't stay around Jupiter for very long. Where do they come from?" Erin quizzed.

"Like most comets, they were once part of the Kuiper Belt, a giant cloud of icy rocks out beyond the orbit of Neptune. Occasionally, one of these Kuiper Belt objects is captured by Neptune's gravity and catapulted toward the sun. As these big chunks of rock and ice fall toward the sun, the sun's heat begins to boil off some of the ice. Like steam rising from a tea-kettle, the vapor streams out behind the rock, forming a tail. And *voila*, the icy rock has become a comet.

"On rare occasions, as these comets pass the orbit of Jupiter, they're captured by Jupiter's gravity and pulled into an orbit around Jupiter. They become Jupiter-family comets.

"The most famous Jupiter-family comet was Comet Shoemaker–Levy, a comet that broke apart, forming a whole string of smaller comets that collided with Jupiter in 1994."

"I remember the pictures of that on NASA's website. It looked incredible."

"It was more incredible than most people can imagine," Michael said, pausing to take another sip of his coffee. "The nucleus of Shoemaker-Levy was probably about three miles across when it exited the Kuiper belt—a gigantic mountain of rock and ice. Sometime in the 1970's, Shoemaker-Levy was captured by Jupiter's gravity and became a Jupiter-family comet.

"In July of 1992, its eccentric orbit brought it too close to Jupiter, and the planet's massive gravity ripped it apart, forming a string of 21 fragments that continued to orbit Jupiter. Two years later, its orbit brought it close to Jupiter again, and the whole train of fragments, some more than a mile in diameter, struck the planet — one-by-one plowing into Jupiter's atmosphere over a period of five days.

"The result was a celestial fireworks display like nothing ever seen before. Hitting the planet at 135,000 mph, the comet fragments exploded with unimaginable fury. Astronomers estimate that the largest of the fragments detonated with the equivalent of 6,000,000 megatons of TNT — that's more than 600 times the total output of our world's nuclear arsenal. It left a scar on Jupiter the size of planet earth."

"If something like that had hit the earth, it would have destroyed our whole planet!"

"Yes, that's the thing astronomers fear most. They call it an E.L.E. An Extinction Level Event. If something like that hit the earth, the human race would be instantly destroyed."

For days, Michael seemed distracted. Then, two weeks later, Erin woke to again find him intently studying something on his iPad.

Erin walked over to him, tightening the belt on her bathrobe. "More news on the comet?"

"Yes," Michael replied without looking up. "Quite a bit, actually.

"As more powerful telescopes have been

trained on it, they discovered that Wormwood is actually a string of two comets, now dubbed Wormwood Alpha and Wormwood Beta.

"Wormwood Alpha is smaller, though still a thousand feet in diameter. It's believed to have broken off of the main body of the comet when its orbit was diverted from Jupiter. Wormwood Beta is a monster, a massive mountain hurtling through space, measuring nearly a mile across.

"They've now announced that Comet Wormwood will not only be visible from the earth, it will come frighteningly close."

"Do they think it might hit the earth?"

"The astronomers assure us that there's better than a ninty-nine percent chance it will miss us entirely, probably passing between the earth and the moon."

"Then why do you look so concerned?"

"Because they're lying." Michael said bluntly. "They know it's going to hit the earth. They're just trying to avoid panic."

"Why do you say that?"

"From Columba's prophecy. This is what he was predicting. I sensed it as soon as Patrick told me about the comet. I just had to wait to be sure.

"Columba warned of stars falling from the sky causing massive destruction on the earth.

"This is what he was describing, and it's why he left us the message.

"We need to call the synaxis together." Michael said finally. "It's time we took a closer look at Columba's prophecy."

Chapter Twenty-One:
Columba's Prophecy Revisited

IONA HOUSE – THE ISLAND OF IONA

That evening, most of the Iona Synaxis met in the main living area of Iona House. Eliel, Rand, Khalil, and Araton came also. Roger and Jamie had been in Inverness for several days helping to establish a new synaxis there, but were expected back on Iona before the evening was out.

Michael shared what was known about the comet, and the reason for his concerns.

"I have a hard time believing this is a natural occurrence," Michael said, glancing at the Irin. "Could the Archons be responsible for this?"

"Before the great wars, the Archons did have spacecraft," Rand said. "But when their cities were destroyed, nearly all of their scientists and engineers were killed. Their civilization collapsed. Their ability to travel through space has been lost for 20,000 years.

"Still, I suppose it's possible that they've recovered some of their ancient technology."

"This is all beginning to fit together," Eliel said thoughtfully.

"The Archons are taking captive millions of humans to form a breeding colony. With their supply of slaves assured, the next step would be to destroy the Earth-realm. Their revenge would be complete."

"Can't we just blast the thing out of the sky?" Lys asked.

"I'm afraid not," Michael shook his head. "Even though we've been warned about this possibility for years, our politicians have not been willing to invest the money to establish that kind of presence in space. About the most we could do now would be to launch a nuke, but this thing is so massive and moving at such a high rate of speed, I doubt it would have much effect. And even if a nuke did break the thing up, the earth would still be destroyed by the rain of comet fragments."

"What about the Irin?" Lys said, turning to Eliel. "Can the Irin do anything to help?"

Eliel shook her head. "The Irin have never developed any spacecraft. The larger moon of Basilea is inhabited, but it's close enough that we can fly there directly. Back before the great wars we had a small spaceport where the Archons traded with us, but we never felt a need to develop craft of our own."

"Isn't there any way to prevent this?" Marissa asked.

"I think there is." Michael responded. "I think that's what Columba's prophecy was written to tell us.

"I've printed off copies of the prophecy for all of us." Michael picked up a sheaf of papers from the floor beside him and handed one to each member.

As Lys skimmed the words of the prophecy, she vividly remembered the day the prophecy had been discovered.

It was right after Jamie's rescue from Hades.

Iona House was still under construction. She'd been having breakfast with Jamie, Erin, and Eliel, along with Holmes and Piper at the St. Columba Hotel.

They'd almost finished when Patrick came running in. "Come quickly! We've found something at the excavation site." The main section of Iona House was nearly complete, but Araton had requested them to enlarge the original plans, adding two additional rooms, so new excavation had begun. Patrick was overseeing the construction.

"What did you find?" Erin asked as they all rose from the table.

"We were excavating for the new foundation when we found what seems to be a small casket or vault. It was buried about three feet down, so it's been there a long time. It has an inscription on the lid. I think it may be some form of ancient Gaelic."

"I'll get Michael and meet you there," Erin responded. "If anyone on the island can read it, it will be Michael."

Fifteen minutes later they had all arrived at the excavation site.

The casket appeared to be carved from native stone, and was still in place at the bottom of the trench, half-buried in the damp, hard-packed soil. The lid was sealed in place with black pitch. Patrick's workmen had carefully brushed the top of the lid free of dirt, revealing an inscription.

Michael eased himself into the trench, then crouched down and traced the letters of the inscription with his index finger as he read. Then he looked up.

"The writing is in ancient Gaelic, but the inscription is very odd."

"How's that?"

"It says, 'The Word of Columba for the Iona Synaxis.'"

They brought in tools and carefully broke the seal. With the seal broken, the lid lifted easily.

Inside the casket, half submerged in dark brackish water, was what appeared to be a block of black stone.

Carefully lifting the object from the casket, the workman carried it into the nearly completed Iona House and rested it on the floor of what would soon be the main living area.

The group crowded around as Michael performed his examination. "This isn't a block of stone at all," he said finally. "It's a heavy object coated with a layer of black pitch. Pitch was often used in the ancient world as a water seal, to protect objects from the elements."

After taking photographs of the object, he began chipping away the thin layer of pitch. The pitch was brittle with age and easier to remove than expected.

Inside, wrapped in thick layers of linen cloth, were a stack of thin gold plates, inscribed with a message from Columba, in ancient Gaelic.

Michael arranged the tablets in order on the floor before him, and looked up at the group.

A hush fell over the room as he began to read.

"This day is the last day of my present life, and on it

I rest after the fatigues of my labor. This night at midnight, I shall go the way of my fathers. For the High King himself has invited me, and in the middle of this night shall I depart, for so it has been revealed to me.

"Soon I will be in Hi-Ouranos, the highest heaven. I will see with my own eyes the twenty-four elders, myriads of angels, the High King, and all of those who have gone before me.

"But before I depart, I must leave this message for those who will come after.

"Iona of my heart, Iona of my love, I know that in days to come, this monastery will be destroyed and the portal allowed to close. The sound of the singers will be replaced by the lowing of cattle and the bleating of sheep. But ere the world come to an end, Iona shall again be as it was.

"A synaxis will form again and the portal will be re-opened, but it will be in a perilous time. I have been shown it in a vision.

"Men and women will fly in the air without wings.

"Every race of mankind will become more wicked and all classes will be addicted to robbery.

"Falsehood and deceit will prevail.

"Great carnage shall be made, justice shall be outraged, multitudinous evils and great violence shall prevail.

"Severe weather and famine shall come. People oppressed for want of food shall pine to death. Dreadful storms shall afflict them. Numberless diseases shall then prevail and remedies will fail.

"Many will regret the days they have lived to see.

"Then a great event shall happen. Stars will fall

from the sky and a deluge shall drown the nations. A more sorrowful event could not possibly happen. The sea at one tide shall rise up and cover Ireland and the green-headed Islay. But Columba's Isle shall rise above the flood.

"To you who find this, I give this word. When you see these events draw near, know that you have entered the time for the restoration of all things. For your world to survive, the Great Portal in the south must again be opened.

"But first must come the restoration. These events may bring total destruction, but they also can bring the restoration of all that was lost. To survive this time, the chosen one must find a way to appear before the High King.

"When the time of crisis comes, do not hesitate. You must go the High King himself. Only in Hi-Ouranos will the answer be found."

Chapter Twenty-Two: Unraveling the Prophecy

IONA HOUSE – THE ISLAND OF IONA

Though everyone in the synaxis realized that Columba's prophecy was significant, the Irin had been strangely unhelpful in providing an interpretation.

Their standard answer was, "When the time comes, you'll know what it means."

From time to time the members of the synaxis would discuss the prophecy, debating the interpretation of certain phrases, but the meaning always remained elusive.

But as they gathered this evening, Michael sensed the meaning was finally coming into focus. After giving everyone time to skim through the prophecy again, Michael began.

"This is Columba's prophecy. Stars falling from the sky, the seas rising up to inundate the land... and with that, the possibility of the total destruction of the earth. I believe Columba's prophecy is describing the Archon's final attempt to destroy the human race. They've established a breeding colony of humans in Hades to ensure their slave supply. Now they plan to obliterate us.

"But I believe Columba has given us the key to survival.

"I've been studying the prophecy for the last

156

several days, and I think the meaning is finally becoming clear.

"The first part of the prophecy is very general. Conditions on earth getting worse. Crime, oppression, violence, severe weather, and incurable diseases. Those are all signs of Archons venting their hatred on the human race.

"But then, after centuries of increasing oppression, the Archons appear to change their tactics. Something truly horrific takes place...

"A great event shall happen. Stars will fall from the sky and a deluge shall drown the nations. A more sorrowful event could not possibly happen.

"I found it interesting that he says *stars* will fall from the sky. That's *"stars,"* plural. More than one object will come out of the sky to threaten us. When I heard that there were two comets headed our way, it confirmed my suspicion that Wormwood was the fulfillment of Columba's prophecy.

"The first result of the falling stars will be a deluge drowning the nations. I believe that describes Wormwood Alpha impacting the earth, probably somewhere in the mid-Atlantic. At a thousand feet in diameter, Wormwood Alpha would produce tidal waves 600 feet tall, pummeling every coastline. Moisture blasted into the atmosphere would unleash a world-wide super typhoon that would cause flooding all over the world.

"Columba describes the effects of the tidal wave on the coast of Ireland, as well as Scotland's Western Isles.

"The sea at one tide shall rise up and cover Ireland

and the green-headed Islay. But Columba's Isle shall rise above the flood.

"I find that last line to be perplexing. As tidal waves batter the Atlantic coastlands they bring great destruction. Ireland is inundated, as is also is the Island of Islay. Islay is the southernmost of Scotland's Western Isles—just 42 miles south of here. But somehow Iona will be able to 'rise above the flood' and survive.

"But apart from Iona escaping the tidal wave, there doesn't seem to be a way to do much about Wormwood Alpha.

"But Columba's prophecy goes on to describe something far worse than tidal waves. A second star is falling from the sky. In describing this next event, he uses the words 'total destruction' and entertains the possibility that the world might not survive. I believe that's a reference to Wormwood Beta. Beta should strike the earth about twenty hours after Alpha, and an impact by a monster that size would destroy the planet.

"But while total destruction is a possibility, Columba tells us that it's not inevitable. The prophecy still seems a bit murky here, but Columba says two things must happen if destruction is to be averted. First, the chosen one must appear before the High King, which will somehow begin the process of restoration."

"Thanks to Roger, we now know what restoration looks like." Marissa said.

"Yes, and I believe the new powers restoration will bring are what will enable us to save the world from destruction. But the restoration is just the first step.

"Columba also says that the Great Portal to the south must be opened. I have no idea what that means, or how it could save the earth from Wormwood Beta.

"So as I see it, this leaves us with five questions:

1. Who is the chosen one?

2. How does the chosen one get to Hi-Ouranos?

3. What does it mean for Iona to rise above the flood?

4. What is the Great Portal in the south?

5. How is total destruction averted?

"Wormwood Alpha and Beta will strike the earth in less than six weeks. We need to be able to answer all five of these questions before that happens."

"I'm curious about the line that talks about Iona rising above the flood." Catherine said.

"Columba says a great flood will inundate Ireland and Islay, but somehow Iona escapes. I don't see how that could happen. I mean, Islay is only 42 miles south of Iona."

"Maybe it's a metaphor." Marissa suggested. "… You know, symbolic language. While destruction will come to much of the world, what you've established on Iona will endure."

"It doesn't sound like a metaphor to me."

Patrick countered. "It sounds like Columba is talking about literal destruction for Ireland and Islay. And that would imply a literal deliverance for this island.

"Do you think it's possible for the tidal wave to be diverted so that it doesn't hit Iona?"

The group was silent for a moment. It was clear that no one had an answer.

"I'm fascinated by the line about the Great Portal to the south," Lys cut in. "Columba links the survival of the world to the re-opening of that portal. Anyone have an idea what that is?"

Patrick looked thoughtful. "The High King told Roger that during the great wars, a massive portal was opened on what is now England's Salisbury Plain, as a means of bringing reinforcements into the Earth-realm. From the perspective of Iona, the Salisbury Plain is far to the south."

Araton spoke. "That portal was eventually taken over by the Archons, and used to transport fresh waves of their warriors to your world. To prevent that, the inhabitants of your realm pulled the portal down.

"The ruined portal still stands on the Salisbury Plain. Today you call it Stonehenge."

Patrick said, "So opening the Great Portal in the south means rebuilding Stonehenge?"

"It would seem so," Araton said.

"But how would rebuilding Stonehenge save the earth?"

"I don't have an answer to that," Araton said, "It sounds like Columba was seeing something we can't yet envision. Remember that Columba's prophecy was given him in a vision directly from the High King. Not even the Irin understand everything in it."

"But the most crucial line in the whole prophecy," Michael interjected, "Is the part about the chosen one. Columba said for the world to survive, the chosen one must appear before the High King.

"So our first big question needs to be, who is the chosen one?"

"Is it Roger?" Lys asked.

"I don't think so," Michael said. "Roger was the first to be restored, but I don't think he's the chosen one. As I remember it, the High King told Roger that the chosen one must *come* to Hi-Ouranos, but at the time Roger was already *in* Hi-Ouranos. I think that eliminates Roger."

They looked at each other with uncertainty. "Is it one of us?"

Araton spoke again, "I believe Erin knows who the chosen one is, but has not been willing to admit it, even to herself."

Erin looked at Araton in perplexity, having no idea what he meant.

"Erin, the day I met you on the rim of the *Halema'uma'u* crater in Hawaii, I told you that you are destined to be a person of great significance. I said you have things within you, abilities you're not yet aware of, that are vital to the future of your world. That's why Pele tried to kill you. I told you that there would come a time when you could save your entire race from destruction."

Araton looked at her for a long moment, then

said, "Erin... *this* is that time."

Erin still stared at him, uncomprehending, tilting her head slightly to the left. Michael reached over and took her hand.

Sensing her perplexity, Araton spoke again, "Erin. Let me say this as clearly as I can. You *are* the chosen one. It is your *destiny* to save your world. You are the only one who can do it."

Erin looked like a deer caught in the head-lights, her eyes wide, unwilling to embrace the truth of Araton's words. She'd long pondered the words of Columba's prophecy, just as had the rest of the synaxis, but she'd never considered the possibility that she could be the one Columba had described.

Araton finally continued. "Columba's word to you is clear, Erin. Do not hesitate. You must go before the High King. As Columba said, *only in Hi-Ouranos will the answer be found.*"

Chapter Twenty-Three: Perilous Journey

IONA HOUSE – THE ISLAND OF IONA

The entire synaxis looked at Erin, stunned by Araton's revelation and waiting for her response.

Erin was silent for a moment, looking down, then brushing a wisp of silky chestnut-brown hair from her face, she again fixed her eyes on Araton. "If you say I'm the chosen one, I'll accept that. I'm willing to do anything it will take to save our world, but I don't have a clue how to do this. How do I get to Hi-Ouranos and what do I need to do when I get there?"

"It sounds like getting there might be the first issue," Michael said. "Columba said you would have to 'find a way' to get there. The implication is that it's not an easy journey. When Roger was describing the human princes who traveled to Hi-Ouranos during the great wars, he described their journey as *heroic*. It's apparently a perilous journey."

"Why would getting to Hi-Ouranos be so difficult?" Erin asked. "We've seen Lys open portals to other dimensions many times. Couldn't Lys just open a portal to Hi-Ouranos?"

"I can answer that," Araton interjected. "Lys can open portals, but only to adjacent dimensions. She can open a portal between the Earth-realm and

Hades, and between the Earth-realm and Basilea.

"But to get to Hi-Ouranos, you would have to pass through seven other dimensions, and that is not an easy journey. You need to first pass through the portal from Iona into Basilea, then travel to a portal that links Basilea and Taveria, which is the next highest dimension. Passing through Basilea would not be difficult. A portal from Basilea to Taveria can be reached in a three hour trek.

"But not all of the realms are as easily traversed. Taveria, for example, is a beautiful world, but much of its surface is covered in rolling ocean. To get to the next portal in Taveria requires a sea voyage of several days.

"Some of the other dimensions you would need to pass through are barely habitable. In Kobuk, for example, the entire realm is in the middle of an ice age, with temperatures far below freezing. The realm of Arenal is experiencing the equivalent of your early Jurassic period. The wildlife you encounter there will be decidedly unfriendly. Traversing Al Naran means crossing a barren, desert wasteland.

"For the Irin, traversing those realms is not a problem. We can fly quickly through inhospitable environments to get from one portal to the next, or even short-cut through the shadow realm in some cases. For an unrestored human, however, this would be a hazardous, time-consuming, and life-threatening journey. Even if the Irin went along to help you, we're talking about a journey that might take you several weeks."

"I have no choice but to try," Erin said. "The

comet will be here in less than six weeks."

"Why don't we all go?" Michael said. "We can travel together. There's strength in numbers."

They all agreed. At this point, they were all ready to lay down their lives to ensure that Erin made it to Hi-Ouranos.

The entire group began to pepper Araton with questions about the realms they would pass through and what provisions they would need to take for the journey.

Just then, the door opened and Roger and Jamie came in. Glancing around and seeing the group already assembled, Roger apologized, "I'm sorry we're late. The plane from Inverness to Oban had mechanical problems, so we missed the earlier ferry to Mull."

After Roger and Jamie found seats, the group quickly filled them in on the situation.

Michael had already begun making a list of the supplies they'd need…. Warm weather gear for the trek across the frozen landscape of Kobuk, supplies of drinking water for the two-day crossing of Al Naran. Catherine, Angus, and Malcom volunteered to come fully armed to offer the group some protection against the unfriendly wildlife of Arenal. The more they planned, the more they appreciated why the journey had been described as heroic.

Roger listened for several minutes while the group described their plans, and finally interrupted.

"Traveling to Hi-Ouranos through a whole series of connecting portals is a risky undertaking, and it's commendable that you are all willing to try it." Roger paused. "But there is another way."

He glanced at Erin, and then to the rest of the group. "I can take you there."

The entire group stared at Roger. Araton and the other Irin looked startled as well.

Glancing at Araton, and then back to Erin, Roger continued. "Let me share a secret not even the Irin here know. When the High King activated my gifts, there was one gift he said would be of supreme importance. He told me I have the ability to open a portal directly into any dimension. That means I can take you directly from Iona to Hi-Ouranos.

"Which means that the journey to Hi-Ouranos does not have to be a perilous one that takes you several weeks," he added. "You can be there in minutes.

"The High King recognized my gift, and knew this time was coming. That's why He sent me back to you. I was sent here for one purpose, to bring Erin to the High King."

For the next hour, the entire group bombarded Roger with questions about Hi-Ouranos and the High King. When he had first returned from Hi-Ouranos, Roger had been reticent to describe what he had seen. Now, for the first time, he opened up.

"Let me try to prepare you for what is ahead," Roger said, fixing his eyes on Erin. "Hi-Ouranos is not like any place you've ever been, or any realm you could even imagine. It doesn't fit into any of our categories.

"The Irin sometimes call it the highest dimension, but that's not totally accurate," he said. "Hi-Ouranos is more than simply the highest dimension. It's a dimension beyond dimensions. All the dimensions we know of are connected there, and beyond Hi-Ouranos uncounted new dimensions open. It's truly the central nexus of the universe.

"Many of the physical laws we're accustomed to don't apply there. From time to time in Hi-Ouranos you catch a glimpse of dimensions that are normally closed to us. You see colors you have never seen before and could never describe.

"You also encounter beings that your physical senses cannot fully comprehend. Our normal experience is limited to three spatial dimensions. But in Hi-Ouranos you'll encounter beings that are native to five and six-dimensional realities. The whole experience is unsettling, but surprisingly, it's not terribly frightening.

"In Hi-Ouranos," he continued, "you will see the ancient ones… a council made up of 24 beings who rule the inhabited realms. Nobody seems to know who they are, or where they came from. But they are highly respected by all the realms.

"More importantly, you will meet the High King. He is a unique being with nearly infinite knowledge and power. And he truly is a king. All the inhabited realms except Hades recognize him as the ultimate authority in the universe.

"I don't know what the High King will do when you get there. I also don't know what he may ask you to do, but I do trust him. I firmly believe that whatever he does will be for our good.

"There's no way to prepare for your journey, and no preparation is necessary. You just need to go. When you get there, the High King will tell you what you need to know."

Erin felt a nameless fear rising within her. She had been to Basilea, and she'd heard the stories of Michael's time in Hades. But both of those dimensions had much in common with the world she knew. Hi-Ouranos was truly the unknown. She glanced at Araton. "Will you go with us?"

"I'd love to," Araton replied, "but I wasn't invited. One doesn't go unbidden into the presence of the King."

"The High King has asked for *you*, Erin. He's the one that gave Columba the prophecy calling for you to come. He also sent Roger back to the Earth-realm to open the way. The High King *wants* you in Hi-Ouranos, and it's imperative that you go quickly."

Chapter Twenty-Four:
The High King

HI-OURANOS – THE HIGHEST REALM

It was decided that Erin would make her journey to Hi-Ouranos the next morning. Roger, of course, would go with her to open the way. Roger related that the High King had also requested that Erin choose four members of the synaxis to accompany her. After a brief discussion, it was agreed that Michael, Jamie, Patrick, and Lys would go.

At 9 AM the next morning, the three couples, accompanied by most of the Iona synaxis, walked down the road from Iona House and climbed the gentle rise to the familiar portal. It was a crisp, cool morning, with a scattering of high clouds overhead.

To the east they could see the medieval monastery, and beyond that, the Sound of Iona and the red granite mountains of Mull. To the west stretched the rugged, green landscape of Iona, and in the far distance, the endless sea. The grass underfoot was splattered with wildflowers.

Somehow the mundane details of Iona seemed almost surreal, as the couples prepared to visit a realm so far beyond their imagining.

Planting their feet on the soft heather between the upright slabs of stone, the couples glanced at each other, and then at the synaxis members who had gathered around them.

"I guess this is it." Erin said nervously. She reached out and took Michael's hand.

Roger took Jamie's hand and gave it a gentle squeeze. "Are we ready?"

"Go for it," said Patrick.

As they all joined hands, each of them nodded their agreement.

Roger began to sing. It was not the soft gentle song they'd all heard Lys sing. It was a song of power.

It rose from deep within Roger and flowed out, syllable after syllable. The words of the song seemed to make no sense, but everyone present knew they carried a meaning far beyond human understanding. The song increased in volume. It had rhythm and meter, and the melody grew more complex. It rose and crested in crescendo after crescendo.

As Roger sang, something happened.

The massive stone slabs atop *Cnoc nan Carnan* began to vibrate, almost imperceptibly at first, but gradually increasing in intensity, until the whole hill seemed to tremble.

Then the hill started to glow. The green heather and the dark earth below turned transparent. The ground became as clear as glass.

Accompanied by a sound like the rumble of distant thunder, a shaft of light shot skyward — a pillar of white light that pierced the clouds overhead. A new wormhole formed — a glowing tunnel that penetrated into the depths of the sky — beyond Basilea, beyond even Taverea, it extended all the way to Hi-

Ouranos, the highest of all realms.

Answering the light from the earth came a light from the heavens. Through the wormhole, a shaft of brilliant light flooded the island of Iona. The light was more than white. It was a shimmering rainbow of blinding radiance, brighter than the brightest day.

When the light finally faded, the three couples were gone.

The couples felt they were flying though a crystal labyrinth of infinite size. Colors flashed around them in beautiful patterns. There was a sensation of incredible speed and a sound like the roar of a thousand Niagaras. It was a breathtaking experience, but it ended quickly. Within moments, they found themselves in Hi-Ouranos.

Reality seemed to shift around them. The scene at first appeared to be a meaningless jumble of colors and shapes. It took a moment for their minds to grasp what they were seeing.

They were standing on a vast plain extending outward to an infinite horizon.

The sky overhead, if it could be called a sky, was like nothing they had ever imagined. It did not feel like they were in an enclosure, yet they knew it was not the vast emptiness of space. Michael had to remind himself that his picture of interplanetary space was an element of their Earth-realm dimension. It might not apply here.

What appeared to be an enormous storm was churning above them, with flashes of lightning and peals of thunder. Though there was no way to accurately judge distances, the storm appeared to be many miles above their heads, and it seemed to extend outward to the horizon. It was in constant motion, whirling slowly around them like a monster hurricane. Yet only a gentle breeze was felt on the vast plain.

In the middle of the eye of the storm was what Michael would later describe as a singularity, a point of brilliant light, infinitely small, yet with a depth great enough to encompass the universe.

It's not a black hole, Michael thought. *A black hole is a singularity that swallows all light and life. This is the opposite.* From this singularity, Michael sensed, all life and light in the universe originated. Michael had the disturbing sense that this singularity might also be sentient. *This is what Eliel once described as the Creator of All Worlds. This is the source of creation.*

Michael glanced around in awe, "Roger was right. This is the dimensional nexus of the universe. There *had* to be a place like this. The place every dimension flows from and is connected."

Directly under the singularity, in the center of the plain, was a huge crystal-clear dais, raised several feet above the surface of the plain.

Surrounding the dais, four fantastic creatures stood at attention. Towering fifteen feet tall, the four sentinels were generally humanoid, though they each had two sets of powerful wings. Their appearance was constantly changing. Michael sensed their bodies occupied more dimensions than his eyes could perceive, and as they moved, different aspects of their being shifted into view.

The effect was like viewing a beautiful diamond with multiple facets. Each movement brought a new facet into view. One minute, a creature's face had the soft gentleness of beautiful woman, but then the facet shifted, and the being was looking at them with the form and fierceness of a large predatory cat. Then its visage morphed again, and the creature had the fiery alertness of an enormous bird of prey. Another shift, and there appeared a powerful beast that defied all description. Each of the facets had its own awesome beauty, but Michael knew the sum total of these creatures' identity went beyond anything his mind could comprehend.

Looking downward, Michael was startled to see that the surface beneath their feet was crystal clear. He had the unnerving impression that he was hovering high in the air. But the dimensions beneath him were shifting also. Experiencing a wave of vertigo, he almost lost his balance.

In one moment, he was looking deep beneath the surface of the world. Peering through thousands of feet of solid rock, he saw an immense crystal cavern that stretched before him as far as he could see. Within the cavern, throngs of small gnome-like creatures were dancing. The beings were short, round, and almost comical in appearance, with short, stubby legs. As they danced, they stomped their thick feet, sending clouds of dust into the air, and waved their chubby arms. The gnomes were in constant motion, stomping and twirling as they joyfully followed each other in a line-dance through the maze-like cavern, winding among deep chasms and around towering crystal spires. The distant *thrum* of their voices seemed to shake the whole cave.

Then suddenly, the scene shifted. Beneath him now was a crystal-clear sea with softly undulating waves. Within the sea, creatures were swimming. He saw great whales and graceful dolphins, but swimming among them were also more fantastic creatures. There were long-necked plesiosaurs leaping above the waves and diving into the depths. There were beings like the mer-folk of human legend — mermaids and mermen — with sinuous, silver-scaled tails and long, flowing human-like hair. All the creatures were cavorting and twirling together in a submarine dance of unbridled delight.

Then the perspective shifted again. And in place of the waves Michael saw beneath him thousands upon thousands of humans — men and women engaged in an intricate, ring-dance around the central dais.

Accompanying their dance, there was music — music unlike anything Michael had ever heard. Every kind of music known to man seemed to join together in a vast symphony. There was the pounding beat of African drums and the sound of a pipe organ blended with the bagpipe and flute. Michael was surprised to hear a violin trace a delicate melody around the piercing wail of an electric guitar. As the music rose to a crescendo, it was accented by the clash of cymbals and the blast of trumpets.

The overall effect was not dissonant and discordant. It was overwhelming beautiful. All the diverse sounds *fit together*, and flowed together in a tapestry of sound that played upon the emotions, producing an irresistible effect of exuberant joy.

Mirroring the throngs around the dais were thousands upon thousands of Irin in the air overhead. They were dancing in the sky, a beautiful, complex dance. Braided streams of Irin flowed in and out, circling the singularity. Others were looping and twirling joyfully above the broad plain. Michael sensed that all the inhabited realms were joining together in a vast celebration.

Around the dais were seven enormous torches, blazing with flames that roared thirty or forty feet into the air.

"I sense the Presence here," Lys whispered. "More than I ever felt it on Iona."

The Presence was intense. It seemed to permeate their bodies, bringing a sense of unparalleled well-being.

Spaced around the dais were twenty-four thrones, mounted on white marble pedestals. On the thrones were the twenty-four ancient ones who ruled the inhabited realms. Had they been standing, each of the creatures would have stood more than twenty feet tall.

They were neither male nor female. Their identity went far beyond any human concept of gender. They were dressed in gleaming white robes, with golden crowns on their heads.

As the three couples approached the dais, they passed among the thrones. Lys looked up at the closest one, and their eyes met. The being did not appear old, just infinitely wise. It seemed strange to Lys, but the brief eye-contact was somehow reassuring. She felt totally secure in the being's presence.

It struck all three of the couples that while Hi-Ouranos was awesome and overpowering, it did not inspire fear.

Shalom, Jamie thought, *there is shalom here! This place feels strange, yet it feels right. I feel like I've always known this place was here. It's like coming home.*

Standing in the middle of the dais, directly below the singularity, was a throne fashioned of an intricately carved, translucent stone. Something like multicolored flames flashed within the throne, and a golden rainbow surrounded it.

Sitting on the throne was a figure that looked like a human being. He was dressed in a simple white robe with a crown of laurel leaves on his head.

As they approached the dais, the man stood to his feet and watched them draw near. Then suddenly the dimensions shifted, and he was no longer on the dais. He was standing right in front of them. He seemed quite ordinary, slightly less than six feet tall, with olive skin and black hair, but there was kindness in his face.

His eyes reflected what Michael described later as an infinite intelligence. Michael sensed that everything in this place, perhaps everything in the universe, was open to his consciousness.

"Hello, Roger," the man said, smiling warmly as he gave Roger a warm embrace. "It's good to see you again. And I'm glad you've brought your friends.

"And Erin, thank you for coming." He reached

out and took her hand, and with a move that surprised everyone, he bowed low and kissed her hand.

One by one, he greeted each of them by name. They all had the sense that the High King already knew them.

The High King paused a minute, then glanced at each of them with a look of great satisfaction.

"This is a time I've long awaited," He said quietly.

"I understand what each of you has gone through to get to this point, and I regret the pain you've experienced on your journey.

"The Archons brought great evil and much suffering into the universe, but it was necessary to allow them to continue in their way for a time, so all the realms could see the true nature of that evil path. But their time is now over. It's time for the universe to be corrected.

"And Erin, you have been chosen.

"The time has come for *everything* to be restored. You have within yourself a very special gift. It's the gift to restore your people."

"What does that mean?" Erin asked tentatively.

"You've seen what restoration looks like. You know Roger.

"He's still the same person you knew before, but in Roger, all of the wounds the Archons inflicted on your race have been healed. He now has the full life-force humans were intended to have, with all the benefit that brings. He will never again know sickness. His life-span stretches before him for hundreds of thousands of years. All of his gifts and abilities have been restored.

"In a few moments, I will restore you as I restored him. Your task will then be to restore the rest of your race. You will begin with the friends you brought here with you. I will show you how. Then, when you return to the Earth-realm, you will restore the rest of your synaxis on Iona. Over time, as the Archons are driven back, you will bring restoration to every member of your race."

He looked at Erin for a long moment.

The scene around them was breathtaking. The storm overhead continued to swirl around the shining singularity. The dimensions shifted and shifted again, bringing into view scenes beyond imagining. The eyes of the ancient ones were all locked on Erin, as were the four sentinels around the dais. But Erin no longer noticed any of that. Her eyes were fixed on the High King.

Finally the High King spoke again. "Erin, are you ready to be restored?"

Erin still had many questions, but in the presence of the King they all seemed insignificant. "Yes," she said simply.

"Then kneel before me."

As Erin knelt, the High King placed his hands on her head, and a shift took place. The entire group felt like they had been transported into a separate reality.

A cloud formed around them, flashing with fire, glowing brightly with the color of amber. Within the cloud, Erin changed. She now appeared to be clothed in a brilliant, golden light, almost too bright to look at directly. Within the golden glow, what appeared to be multicolored flames were in constant motion, shifting in kaleidoscopic patterns across and around her body.

And then the cloud dissipated and the light faded.

They were standing again on the infinite plain at the foot of the crystal dais.

Erin and the High King stood face to face, looking at each other.

"Erin, your life force has been restored, and your gifts activated.

"But there is one more thing you need to complete your mission. When you are sent out to accomplish a difficult task, it's never good to be alone. I'd always intended you to have a co-worker—a friend who could complement your gift."

The High King waved his hand and the sky parted, and beyond it was a realm beyond realms. Erin knew the realm she was seeing was not any of the realms accessible from earth. It had a beauty she could not describe, and colors she'd never seen before. And it was occupied. There were people, some of them winged, flying with great freedom through a landscape that defied description.

One of the beings flew through the portal the High King had opened. Erin felt it was the most beautiful creature she had ever seen. Though she had no wings, the being flew effortlessly, surrounded by a golden glow. She was dressed in a pale green garment that seemed as light as gossamer. Long walnut-brown hair feathered softly behind her as she descended to a graceful landing a few feet in front of Erin. The woman's features were delicate and her skin fair, almost translucent. As her golden glow faded, she looked at Erin and smiled warmly.

The High King glanced at the new arrival, and then back to Erin. "Erin, let me introduce you to *Sylvia.*

"Syl is from your world, and was always intended to be part of your destiny. Her gift was designed to work with yours, to assist you in your task, but she was stolen away from you. But she has consented to come back to aid you in the work ahead.

"As your gifts work together, your task will become much easier. You have the ability to restore the human life-force. Sylvia has the ability to instantaneously activate gifts."

Sylvia... Erin thought, staring at the radiant being standing in front of her. *There's something familiar about her.*

Then Erin remembered. "Sylvia *Romano?*"

"Yes." The woman smiled. "That's me."

"I *remember* you!" Erin said, tears welling in her eyes, thinking of the morning she'd watched and rewatched the security camera's grainy video of Sylvia's death. "When you were killed, I felt such a sense of loss. I wept for hours. I knew we were somehow connected.

"What happened to you?"

"I made some terrible choices during my time in the Earth-realm," Sylvia said, "and the Archons captured me.

"They imprisoned me in one of their strongholds where they beat me, starved me, raped me, and kept me drugged. Then, when I was worn down enough, Kariena possessed by body and turned me into a walking bomb.

"Kareina actually thought she had destroyed me, but she didn't realize that death is never the end. Life always continues.

"The moment Kariena's bomb tore my body apart, I found myself with the High King. He brought me to a wonderful realm. It was a place more beautiful than anything I've ever imagined. I never wanted to leave, but he told me that my work in the Earth-realm was not yet complete.

"I've been waiting there for you. I'm ready to go with you now and fulfill my destiny."

"Sylvia's death was a terrible loss to your world," the High King said. "But the time has come when every loss can be restored.

"And now," the High King said, "It's time for you and Sylvia to restore your friends."

The high King waved his hand and the amber cloud, flashing with fire, formed around them again. At a signal from the High King, Erin's friends drew close. Michael was the first. As Erin placed her hands on her husband's head, Sylvia placed her hands on his back. And the transformation began.

Chapter Twenty-Five: Preparing for the Comet

THE ISLAND OF IONA

Comet Wormwood was scheduled to strike the earth in a little more than two weeks. It was clearly visible in the sky now, a bright, fuzzy dot with a graceful, glowing tail streaming behind it for hundreds of thousands of miles.

Amateur astronomers were ecstatic. Telescope purchases boomed. Many enthusiasts scheduled comet watching parties. Astronomy websites were filled with beautiful pictures of the shining comet as it approached. There was still no hint in the news of the disaster ahead.

By this time, all of the Iona Synaxis members had experienced restoration. Roger was working with the Irin to help each of them acclimate to their new gifts. There were many skills to acquire.

They all had to learn to enter and exit the shadow realm, enabling them to bypass physical barriers. They learned to open rifts in the atmosphere, allowing them to travel to any location within a given realm, almost instantly.

One of the hardest skills to master was the ability to fly. They had no wings as the Irin did, but when their life-force was activated, it could thrust them forward in flight in a way that rivaled anything the Irin could do.

"This is like a *flying* dream!" Michael exclaimed the first time he tried it. "Moving through the air by *will* alone! Most people have dreams of being able to fly like this," he added. "When they wake up, there is always a sense of disappointment that it's not real. Only this *is* real!"

Michael hovered in midair, then swooped down almost to the ground and flew horizontally across the Bay at the Back of the Ocean, before shooting upward to make a smooth landing on *Dun I*, the tallest hill on Iona.

In addition to mastering the joys of flight, there were individual gifts to be learned. All of the gifts they had exercised as synaxis members now operated at a dramatically new level of power. And there were also new gifts. Ones they had never experienced. One of the gifts that aroused the most excitement was the gift of *telekinesis*, the ability to levitate objects and move them through the air without touching them.

On the second evening after the restoration had begun, Marissa Kobani was sitting with Lys in the main living area enjoying the nightly wine and cheese buffet with Erin and Sylvia, when Roger came in and sat down across from them.

Seeing Roger, Marissa smiled, "Roger, we've just been talking about the restoration. It is so incredible, it seems like a dream! I can hardly believe it's real.

"I'll always remember that day when you showed up in the sheikh's dungeon with your life-force glowing! Talk about the cavalry riding over the hill to the rescue! I had no idea what you were, but what you did amazed me.

"And now it's happened to me! I can do the same things you did! I spent most of the afternoon today *flying!*"

Marissa had been one of the first volunteers to be restored when the three couples returned from Hi-Ouranos. She'd stood between Erin and Sylvia and in the midst of a glowing cloud, had been transformed.

Marissa looked at Syliva and smiled. "When I woke up this morning, I feared I'd dreamed it all! Then I activated my life-force and my whole body was clothed in the golden glow. Standing beside my bed, I willed myself to rise, and rose several inches above the floor. I was so startled, I let my life-force fade and fell back to the floor. But it was enough. I knew it was real. All day, I've felt a sense of joy and well-being I've never known in my life.

"One thing I have to ask," she said, turning back to Roger. "Are you certain this is permanent? I mean, when I wake up tomorrow morning, this won't be gone will it?"

"I assure you, Marissa, it's permanent. You are changed forever. Your new abilities will be there tomorrow, next week, next month, and twenty-thousand years from now."

Marissa looked perplexed for a moment, then a look of amazement came across her face and her eyes filled with tears. "That's right! I'd forgotten that part! I'm no longer doomed to grow old and die in forty or fifty years. I'll still be here tens of thousands of years from now. This is overwhelming!"

"And not only will your gifts still be here," Roger added. "They'll grow. Right now they're in an embryonic form. But as you practice exercising your gifts, you'll gain skill and the gifts will strengthen. You'll be amazed at the things you'll be doing even a few months from now."

"Talking about gifts," Marissa dabbed at her tears with a napkin and grinned. "Let me show you something else I can do!"

Marissa extended her right hand toward the half-full wine bottle on the coffee table. For a moment, nothing happened. Then very slowly, the bottle began to slide across the glass surface. Marissa stopped and looked up at Roger. "I can move things without touching them!"

"That's called telekinsesis." Roger said. "I call people with that gift 'movers.' They move things by thought alone. It's a wonderful gift. I can do it a little myself. I'd encourage you to keep practicing with it. If that gift is surfacing this quickly after your restoration, you probably have a high-level gifting."

In response to Roger's encouragement, Marissa turned back to the wine bottle and extended her hand. After several unsuccessful attempts, Marissa succeeded in raising the bottle several inches above the table, moved it about a foot through the air, then spun it slowly around before resting it on the table again. "You do to have an unusual ability!" Roger laughed. "Keep working on that!"

Marissa beamed with the excitement of a little

child opening presents on Christmas morning. For several minutes she tried moving the bottle around, testing her ability to control it.

"Do you know what this means?" She said finally, looking at Lys with a twinkle in her eye. "It means I'll never again have to ask someone to pass the wine!"

As if to demonstrate, she levitated the wine bottle ten inches into the air, moved it about a foot closer, then tilted it, allowing a rich stream of Cabernet Sauvignon to pour into her glass.

While all of them felt a giddy excitement in discovering their new gifts and abilities, there was also a dead seriousness. Every member of the synaxis knew the world was scheduled for termination in just two weeks, and that their ability to discover and use their gifts might be the key to its survival.

In spite of their new gifts, day-to-day life for the synaxis members had changed very little. They still all met for breakfast each morning at Iona House.

"So where are you going today?" Lys asked as she and Patrick sat down across from Michael, Erin, and Sylvia.

"I'm flying down to Stonehenge again to check out my latest theories," Michael said. "I've been studying the ancient portal for weeks, but there's nothing like being there in person. And having the ability to fly makes it unbelievably easy to get there. If I shortcut through the shadow realm, I can be there in twenty minutes!"

"Why not just open a rift?"

"I'm still not very skilled in that," Michael laughed sheepishly. "Sometimes I end up in odd places. Last week I tried opening a rift to London and ended up in the middle of the Sahara Desert!

"Besides, I really enjoy flying. It was a childhood dream."

Just then, Casey walked up to take their breakfast orders. When they'd finished putting in their requests, Patrick looked at Erin and Sylvia. "And what about you two?"

"We're going down to Manchester today," Erin smiled. "Several of the Manchester area synaxis groups have scheduled a time to meet together, so we're going to attempt another group restoration. We hope to be able to see more than a hundred synaxis members restored by the end of the day.

Lys looked surprised. "I had no idea you could do that."

"We did our first group restoration in Edinburg and it was surprisingly easy. Since then we've done it in several other cities. Doing group restorations has greatly multiplied the number of people we see restored."

"With the comet strike just weeks away," Sylvia added. "We're feeling an urgency to see as many people transformed as possible."

"How do you train the people to use their new gifts?" Patrick asked.

"Roger and I have worked out a plan," Sylvia said. "Once I activate their gifts, I teach the people how to open a rift to Iona. With that mastered, they can travel to Iona as often as necessary, for Roger to help them develop their gifts. Jamie has already begun a database to keep track of who has which gifts!"

"I think Roger and Jamie will have their hands full!" Erin laughed. "Counting the restorations we did in northern Scotland, we now have close to a thousand people restored. We hope to start restoring several thousand a week."

"Have you made any more progress in interpreting the prophecy?" Lys asked, changing the subject.

"We still have no idea what it means for Iona to rise," Erin said, "or how restoring the Great Portal to the south can save the earth, but Michael is working to find out all he can about Stonehenge."

Chapter Twenty-Six: The Announcement

THE ISLAND OF IONA

Two weeks from impact, the announcement was finally made. It was the most horrifying moment in human history. A panel of eminent scientists appeared on a news conference carried by every network. The broadcast was simultaneously translated into every language on earth. The basic announcement could be summed up in one sentence: "Our world will be destroyed in two weeks."

The rest was just details.

As Michael had anticipated, Wormwood Alpha was predicted to strike in the mid-Atlantic, creating a massive tidal wave that would spread outward in all directions. Michael shuddered at the thought that in two weeks, cities like New York, Boston, Lisbon, and Miami would no longer exist. Everyone living in coastal areas was urged to evacuate.

Not that it would do much good. Twenty hours after Wormwood Alpha struck, Wormwood Beta would hit.

Beta's impact zone had been narrowed to an area of fifty square miles, about ninety miles south-west of London, England. There was no way to divert it. The earth was doomed. Wormwood Beta would hit with such overwhelming force that the explosion would literally rip the planet apart. It was an Extinction Level Event. There could be no survivors.

The entire synaxis had gathered in the main living area to watch the announcement. As the head of the Royal Observatory continued his droning explanation of the destruction to come, a map of England was displayed on the screen, with the projected impact zone outlined in red.

Michael studied it for a moment, then glanced at Patrick in amazement. "Do you see what's right in the middle of the impact zone?"

"I do," Patrick answered. "That can't be a coincidence."

"What is it?" Lys asked.

"The impact zone." Patrick replied. "The area outlined in red on that map is the Salisbury Plain!"

"Isn't that where Stonehenge is located?" Casey asked.

"Exactly!" said Michael "In fact, Stonehenge is almost dead center on the impact zone."

Patrick looked from Lys to Michael. "Are you both thinking what I'm thinking?"

"Columba had it all figured out!" Michael beamed.

"That's how the earth escapes destruction! If a large enough portal can be opened above Stonehenge, Wormwood Beta will enter the portal before it hits our atmosphere. The comet will go through the wormhole and be instantly transferred out of this dimension without striking the earth."

"Where would it go?" Erin asked.

"Araton said when it was last used, the portal had been linked to Hades."

"So instead of striking the earth, the comet will pass through the wormhole to Hades, instantly destroying the Archon home-world."

"Do we have a right to do that?"

"I don't see that we have a choice."

"We don't know how to retune a portal to a different location, and there's no time to learn. And remember, this whole thing was the Archons' idea. But their plan has backfired. It's their world that will be destroyed.

"When we open the Stonehenge portal, Wormwood Beta will go straight to Hell."

The Great Portal in the South

Chapter Twenty-Seven:
The Great Portal in the South

IONA HOUSE – THE ISLAND OF IONA

That evening, Michael met with Patrick, Lys and Erin in the main living area to share what he'd learned about Stonehenge.

"Stonehenge was the largest and most complex portal ever constructed," he said. "Archaeologists have long known that it was built in several stages, and now we know why. Let me show you." Michael called up a series of pictures on his iPad.

"The earth was in the midst of a devastating war with the Archons, and our leaders appealed to Hi-Ouranos for help, so the ancient ones put out a call for volunteers to defend our world. To enable that, a large portal needed to be built. That was Stonehenge.

"The first stones set in place were a ring of 45 'bluestones' — named because of their blue-grey appearance. These bluestones are columns of stone that weigh up to four tons each, and were brought to the Salisbury Plain from the Preselli Mountains, in southwest Wales."

Michael tapped a small arrow on the right side of the iPad's screen, and a ring of 45 upright blue-stones appeared on the Salisbury Plain.

"That reminds me a lot of the portal at Loch Buie," Patrick said with a shudder, remembering his vigil at the Loch Buie portal as he waited for Lys to return from Hades.

"It was a pretty typical stone circle," Michael agreed, "though larger than most. Portals similar to this had been built in a number of places.

"But a portal like this can only transport a few dozen people at a time," Michael continued, "So as the Great Wars intensified, it was evident that the portal needed to be expanded. Massive sarsens — great sandstone boulders — were brought in from the Marlborough Downs, 20 miles to the north.

"These sarsen stones were huge, weighing 25 tons each and standing 18 feet high. Thirty of them were placed in a circle around the bluestones. Then stone lintels, weighing seven tons each, were lifted into place to connect the tops of the uprights."

Michael tapped the screen again, and a ring of tall upright stones appeared around the bluestones. He tapped again, and lintels faded into view, linking the tops of the uprights and forming a continuous circle of stone twenty feet in the air.

"The ring of sarsens enabled the wormhole to be enlarged so hundreds of people could come through the wormhole at a time. They quickly found, however, that a portal that size tends to be unstable, so another detail was added. Within the bluestones, a horseshoe formation of still larger blocks were added. Called 'trilithons,' they each consisted of two twenty-five foot tall sarsens, joined by a massive stone lintel."

Michael tapped the screen once more, and a horseshoe of five tall trilithons appeared in the middle of the bluestone ring. "The horseshoe of trilithons stabilized the wormhole and allowed the portal to operate at full capacity."

"The trilithons are all shaped like the Greek letter *pi*," Patrick observed.

"A lot of people have noticed that," Michael smiled. "I'm not completely sure how the portal worked, but it evidently did. The Great Portal at Stonehenge allowed hundreds of thousands of people to be transported between the dimensions in a very short amount of time."

Michael tapped the screen once again, and a number of outlying stones appeared on the northwest corner of the portal.

"These 'station stones' were erected to tune the portal to a specific location. With those in place, the 'Great Portal in the south' was ready for operation!"

Erin and Patrick studied the final image Michael had called up.

"That's very impressive," Patrick said,

"It doesn't look very much like Stonehenge today, Erin observed. I didn't realize how much damage had been done over the years."

"At some point during the Great Wars," Michael responded, "as the tide of battle swung toward the enemy, the Archons captured the Stone-henge Portal and linked it to the Great Portal of Abadon. As Araton told us, the Archons began using it to bring a massive new invasion force into the Earth-realm. To halt this, the local inhabitants pulled Stonehenge down.

"Over the centuries, the purpose of the stones was forgotten. Many of the stones were scavenged for building materials—reused for Roman buildings and medieval churches in the vicinity.

"What we see today is just a faint memory of what Stonehenge had originally been.

"In fact, what we have today is a mess." Michael shook his head as he tapped the screen again, calling up a picture of Stonehenge as it is now.

"Only six lintels remain in place on the sarsen stone circle, with two more lying on the ground. Only three of the five trilithons are intact. Four of the uprights from the sarsen circle are missing entirely

"So rebuilding Stonehenge means more than just setting fallen blocks back in place. It means quarrying new bluestones in Wales and new sarsens from the Marlborough Downs and somehow transporting these multi-ton boulders to the Salisbury Plain."

As Patrick and Erin looked at each other with concern, Michael added, "And we have less than two weeks to do it."

The next morning, Michael and Erin were eating breakfast with Sylvia when Patrick and Lys came in, a look of excitement on their faces. As they took their seats, Patrick began. "I've been thinking about the problem of rebuilding Stonehenge and I believe I have a solution.

"Finding new stones to replace the ones that had been lost seemed like an insurmountable obstacle. I struggled with it most of the night. If we had six months, it might be possible, but to quarry the stones and transport them here in less than two weeks by normal means simply cannot be done.

"I'd thought of casting replacements in concrete, but the original builders seemed to be very specific about the kind of stones they used. They transported the bluestones 250 miles from Wales to the Salisbury Plain, when they could have easily quarried another kind of stone locally. A substitute might not work.

"I was still wrestling with the problem when the sun came up, so I went for a walk on the beach to clear my mind.

"On the north end of the island, I saw Marissa practicing with her gift."

While Michael, Erin, and Sylvia listened in fascination, Patrick described his early morning encounter with Marissa.

"I'd just rounded the north end of the island when I saw Marissa standing on the beach near the tide-line, casually toying with what must have been a ten-ton boulder.

"Standing thirty feet from the rock, Marissa pointed a finger in its direction and willed it to rise. Without hesitation, the boulder rose up from the beach and hovered several feet in the air. She held it there for a moment and gently set it back down, then raised it even higher, moved it fifty feet down the beach, and set it down again.

"The sight of it boggled my mind," Patrick laughed. "I mean, here's Marissa Kobani, who can't weigh more than 120 pounds herself, manhandling this huge rock as though it were a pebble.

"The sight was so incongruous, I couldn't help but applaud."

"Marissa, that's incredible!"

"Hi, Patrick!" Marissa grinned, her luxuriant raven hair rustling softly in the early morning breeze. "I didn't see you there."

"Marissa, what you just did was incredible! I had no idea you could do that!"

"I was having trouble sleeping so I thought I'd come out and do an experiment. I've been working the last few days on developing my gift. Up to this point, I've focused on precise handling. Moving small objects... and of course, pouring wine!" She laughed.

"But it occurred to me that I've never tested to see how much I can actually lift.

"The hardest part has been finding something big enough to challenge my abilities. Last night I tried lifting the Hummer a few feet into the air. It was a piece of cake. No effort at all.

"So this morning I remembered all the huge boulders scattered around on the beach here at the north end of the island."

"It looked like you handled that one pretty easily."

"It took a little more concentration, but it really was not hard. I don't think I'm even close to the limits of my ability."

She turned to an even larger rock, half buried in the sand. With a flick of her wrist, the boulder shook, rocked back and forth for a few seconds, then eased into the air, a trail of sand and seaweed sloughing off its sides. With a playful look in her eye,

Marissa held the massive boulder twenty feet in the air and started it tumbling end over end. Loose sand sprayed from it in all directions. She finally steadied it and rested it back down on the beach again.

"I wish I'd had this ability when I was in the sheikh's palace!" She laughed, enjoying a mental image of the sheikh suspended in mid-air, screaming in terror, as he began tumbling end over end. "I could have definitely livened things up in his playroom!"

"I stood with Marissa for 20 minutes as she continued to test the limits of her gift," Patrick said. "Larger stones were a bit harder for her to control, but I think that may be a matter of practice. So far as I can tell, if she wills an object to move, it moves. On the scale we're dealing with, size and weight seemed inconsequential.

"It's true that Marissa is unusually strong with her telekinesis gift, but I've heard that a number of synaxis members now have similar abilities. I texted Jamie, and she told me she already has close to three hundred people in the database with telekinesis gifts just as strong as Marissa's.

"Geologists have known for years the exact locations where the original rocks for Stonehenge were quarried," Patrick continued. "With enough people like Marissa, it should be possible to quarry replacement stones at the original locations and transport them to Stonehenge in less than a week."

Seeing the truth of Patrick's proposal, Erin quickly texted both Jamie and Marissa. A meeting was set to begin planning the reconstruction of

Stonehenge.

The announcement of the comet's "ground zero" site had brought a spontaneous mass evacuation from the region around the Salisbury Plain. People somehow felt driven to escape the impact point.

The rebuilding of Stonehenge began without incident.

Chapter Twenty-Eight: To Raise Iona

MARTYR'S BAY PUB – THE ISLAND OF IONA

After the announcement of the earth's destruction, things seemed relatively normal for several days. Everyone who heard the broadcast was stunned. The beautiful comet in the sky had now become a hammer of destruction hanging over their heads, about to strike. Telescopes were trashed and comet watching parties were canceled.

Many sat and wept for days. Families clustered together. Young couples forgot everything else and sought comfort in each other's arms. Many just got drunk. It seemed the world was taking its death sentence with unusual calmness.

Then, on the fourth day, it all fell apart. There were riots in the streets. Gangs began looting and raping in every city. The realization had hit that there were no longer consequences for any action, so everyone did whatever they felt like doing. Driven by frustration and rage, what many apparently felt like doing was to try to destroy the world before the comet did.

The goal of the Archons had finally been realized. Highways out of Atlantic coastal cities were in total gridlock. As fuel supplies ran out, thousands were stranded. Tempers flared. Riots spread to more and more cities. Civilization had begun to unravel.

Nine days before the comet strike, Patrick, Lys and Marissa were eating lunch with Michael and Erin in the Martyr's Bay Pub when Jamie walked in. Marissa had just finished giving them a progress report on the quarrying of the new blocks for Stonehenge.

"Michael, can I talk to you?" Jamie said.

"Certainly. Is this something the rest of the group can hear?"

"They're fine," Jamie said as she nervously pulled up a chair.

"Can I get you a drink?"

"Not right now. I just need to share with you what I've been thinking.

"I have an idea," she said. "It's a crazy idea. It's an insane idea. But I think it may be right.

"I've been pondering the line in Columba's prophecy about Iona rising above the flood. I'm not completely certain what that means, but I think it might be literal. I believe we may be able to temporarily raise the island of Iona so the tidal wave will not destroy it."

"How could we do that?"

"You know that the surface of the earth rests on a series of tectonic plates, great slabs of stone that float on the earth's molten core. Roger told us that during the great wars, the Archons had a technology using sound to soften these tectonic plates and reshape earth's surface. Whole continents sank while others rose. I think something like that might be possible here, on a smaller scale. If we could lift the tectonic plate under Iona just six hundred feet, Iona could literally rise above the flood.

"I suppose that's possible," Michael said, "at least theoretically, but we don't have that Archon technology."

"But we do have singers," Jamie rejoined. "Even with the limited powers the singers had before the restoration, they could produce dramatic effects. We've known for a long time that singers can do more than just open a portal. Catherine told us the story of how she sang over Angus and his broken leg healed. Singers have the power to transform matter by the sound of their voice.

"In the light of that, I believe we may have a way to save Iona."

"This may sound like a silly question," Marissa said, "but apart from the fact that we happen to live here, why is it so important to save Iona? I mean, I do love this place, but with so much of the earth being devastated, why is it so important to save this island?"

"I'm not sure I understand it all either," Jamie said, "but it seemed to be very important to Columba. He sensed there was something unique about this place. When he describes Iona rising above the flood, I get the impression that he considered it a terribly important event."

"Remember that Iona is a 'thin' place," Michael said. "It's the only place on earth were a wormhole to Basilea can be continuously maintained. If we lose

Iona, we'll lose the Iona portal. We could still have intermittent communication with Basilea, but our permanent connection would be lost.

"I'm not sure what conditions will be like on earth after the comet strike, but I suspect that our link with Basilea might be more important than ever."

"I agree with Michael," Erin said. "I've felt for a long time that Iona is more crucial to the future of our world than we know. If it's at all possible to save it, we should not let this island be destroyed."

Michael glanced at Jamie, "So tell me what you are envisioning."

"Picture a 600-foot tall tidal wave approaching the British Isles. It first inundates Ireland, though the tall cliffs along Ireland's western shore will save a lot of the island from destruction. As it moves eastward, the tidal wave next inundates the little island of Islay. Islay is the southernmost of the western isles, just 40 miles south of Iona.

"Yet as the tidal wave approaches Iona, something happens. Columba said that Iona will rise above the flood and be spared. I wondered how Islay could be inundated yet Iona escape destruction.

"Then I looked at the geology of the British Isles and found something interesting. There's a major earthquake fault that runs right across Scotland. It's called the Great Glen Fault. It's like a giant crack that runs arrow-straight from the Firth of Lorne on the southwest to Inverness on the northeast. Loch Ness, home of the legendary lake monster, is actually part of the Great Glen system.

"The crack is the result of the collision of two

tectonic plates, the Laurentia and Baltic. These slabs of rock are literally floating on the sea of molten rock that makes up the core of the earth, and they appear to be locked in a battle. The plate on the north side of the fault is slowly sliding to the northeast, while the plate to the south is trying to move to the southwest.

"What's significant is where it's located, with respect to Iona. The fault cuts across Scotland, just south of Iona, but just north of the Island of Islay. Islay is on the one tectonic plate, and Iona is on the other.

"When the tidal wave hits, Islay will bear the brunt of the destruction. There's no way to escape it, though the authorities should be able to evacuate the population. But if the southern edge of Iona's tectonic plate can be temporarily raised by at least 600 feet, Iona and the rest of northern Scotland could be spared."

"Jamie, if I didn't know your IQ, I'd say you were crazy," Erin laughed. "But I know you've thought this through. I'm hesitant to doubt your conclusion."

Erin looked at Lys. "You're the most experienced singer we have. What do you think?"

"It's worth a try," Lys answered. "I don't see what we have to lose."

Erin then glanced at Michael.

He shrugged his shoulders in response. "I agree. I think this is worth a try."

Erin looked thoughtful for a moment, then asked Jamie, "How many singers do we have in our database now?"

"Close to five hundred."

"Do all of the singers know how to access the shadow realm?" Erin asked.

"I think so."

Erin was silent for a moment, then made her decision. "Contact the singers and have them meet you on Iona. Schedule them to work in shifts, entering the shadow realm and descending to the boundary between the tectonic plates. Let's see what they can do."

"It may not work," Jamie cautioned. "In fact, it seems pretty farfetched. All we have to go on is a cryptic line in Columba's prophecy."

"But," Erin said, "at this point, it's the only option we have."

"Can I say something," Patrick interjected as Jamie left.

They all gave him their attention.

Patrick looked deeply troubled. "I keep thinking about the millions of human slaves in Hades. I'm still having that dream every night and it's horrible. Is there any way to rescue them before the comet hits?"

Michael was silent for a moment. "I've been pondering your dream, Patrick," he said thoughtfully. "I believe you've been given that dream for a reason, and perhaps this is it. If there is any way to rescue those captives, we'll try."

"We've got to find a way," Patrick insisted. "If what I see in the dream is accurate, the condition of those slaves is horrendous beyond belief. Every night

I see new details.

"When Eliel first talked about the Archons starting a breeding colony, I pictured families living in little cubicles. That's not what is happening.

"Right now, the human slaves are all still crammed together in the big crater. Some of them have been living there close to two years. The younger women are forced to sleep in pens where they're repeatedly raped by the guards until they become pregnant. When children are born, they're placed in the care of older women while the younger women are returned to the pens to be impregnated again. The Archon's goal is for every healthy woman to be almost continually pregnant. The older women are forced to work in filthy, factory-like nurseries where children are brought up as obedient slaves for their Archon masters.

"During the day, both men and women are organized into work crews, building hydroponic tanks in huge empty caverns. Others are slaving in the intense heat, carving new tunnels and passageways to provide living space for the rapidly expanding human population.

"In the crater, filth is everywhere. There are no bathing facilities. There is no privacy, and the stench is overwhelming.

"And all the people are held in perpetual terror by the banshees. Banshees continually soar above the crater, dropping down to seize victims without warning.

"The strangest thing of all is that the man who seems to be in charge of the whole operation is someone whose name I recognized. It was Grat Dalton."

"It sounds like Kareina finally found a job for Grat that fits his personality," Erin mused. "The whole plan sounds like something Grat might have thought up."

She shook her head as she remembered the encounters she'd had with Grat at Rex's ranch. "Grat Dalton has always been a psychopath—cold, brutal, with no trace of compassion. I feel sorry for any slaves that come under his influence."

"Erin, we must find a way to rescue those people."

"Patrick, we'll save as many captives as we can," she responded. "But our top priority is to save the world."

Chapter Twenty-Nine: Into the Depths of the Earth

BENEATH THE ISLAND OF IONA
START HERE

Lys was put in charge of the attempt to raise Iona, since she was the most experienced singer. Before she led others into the depths of the earth, however, she decided to take a scouting trip, and invited Catherine to accompany her.

Sipping a glass of wine after lunch that afternoon, Lys explained what they would attempt to do. "Iona, along with the rest of northern Scotland, rests on a gigantic slab of rock called a tectonic plate. Islay, and the lands to the south rest on a different plate. These plates are actually floating on an ocean of molten rock.

"To try to raise Iona, we'll have to enter the shadow realm and descend to the level of the plates, then try to locate the fault line between Iona's plate and Islay's. Once we locate that boundary, we'll see if our gifts have any effect on them."

Catherine hesitated for a moment. "I need to be honest with you, Lys. I'm not very familiar with the shadow realm.

"I've been there once but it was pretty much by accident," she explained. "I'd been experimenting with my new powers when everything around me suddenly got vague and ethereal and sort of transparent. I found it a wee bit unsettling—it seemed like I was drifting helplessly in space. I almost panicked before I figured out how to get out. I told Roger about it and he said I'd been in the shadow realm.

"So it's true that I've *been* to the shadow realm, but I'm not quite sure how I got there or how to get there again, and I have no idea how to function once I'm there. So if I'm going to do this with you, I'm going to need a bit of coaching."

"No problem," Lys laughed. "I'll walk you through it. The shadow realm is really easy once you get a feel for it."

They quickly finished their wine, then stood together in the center of the room.

"Let's start by slipping into the shadow realm."

Trying to remember what she'd done the last time, Catherine willed herself to enter the shadow realm. Nothing happened.

"It's not working."

Catherine gritted her teeth and tried again. And then again.

Still nothing.

"Relax." Lys smiled reassuringly, seeing the frustration on Catherine's face. "It really doesn't take a lot of effort. It's like taking a step, but not in a direction you know. The shadow realm is part of our world, but it's shifted out of the plane we normally access.

"Try it one more time, but this time actually take a step forward. As you do, will yourself to exit the realm you know."

Catherine tried again, willing herself to step out of her world. This time, there was a sensation of movement, but not in a direction she could identify. Glancing around, it didn't look like she'd moved, yet the room around her had somehow faded. It seemed like a ghostly outline of the world she knew.

Lys was right beside her. "You did it! You've made it into the shadow realm.

"Now, look around you. You're on the very edge of the dimension you've always lived in. You can still see everything, but you're shifted slightly out of our normal reality."

"It feels like I'm outside the world looking in."

"That's a good description of it."

"Since there's nothing material here, slipping into the shadow realm allows us to pass through material objects. It's handy for passing through walls and doors. The key for us right now is that it will give us access to the depths of the earth. In the shadow realm, there's no solid ground beneath our feet, so we can descend to the level of the tectonic plates."

Looking down, Catherine realized for the first time that there truly was nothing solid under her feet. It felt like she was suspended in mid-air.

Resisting an urge to panic, she willed herself to relax. As the initial shock wore off, she found that the experience was actually quite pleasant. It felt like she was floating in a crystal-clear pool of water.

"To get around in the shadow realm, you use your life-force, just like do when you're flying. If you will yourself to rise, you rise. If you will yourself to descend, you go down. You can travel in any direction. It's really sort of fun."

Lys gave Catherine time to practice using her life-force to move in different directions, gaining control of her speed and direction.

"Now let's try going down," Lys said.

Willing themselves to descend, they drifted down through the floor of Iona House.

"This is strange..." Catherine said as she descended, sounding more confident. "I know I'm underground, but I can still see in every direction. It's like looking at the earth with x-ray vision."

They could see every detail of the ground beneath Iona House.

At first, they were surrounded by sand and hard-packed soil, interspersed with large rocks. As they continued to descend, the hard-pack soil gave way to layer after layer of solid rock.

Descending still further, they passed through an immense water-filled cavern system. Branches of the cave stretched as far as they could see, and some of the caverns were huge. A few of the passages had great fish swimming languidly through them.

"This is amazing," Catherine said. "I've lived here all my life but never knew Iona had caves."

"This surprises me too. I guess the only way a cave ever gets discovered is if a branch happens to extend up to the surface. Since none of these caves connect to our world, there's no way we'd know they were here.

"It might be like this everywhere on earth," Lys mused. "The ground beneath our feet could be literally honeycombed with caverns we were never aware of."

As they went deeper, the caves narrowed to tiny fissures. Rocks fused together, becoming darker, and visibility was cut to a few hundred feet.

They passed thick seams of coal and occasional deposits of iron pyrite and crystalline quartz.

It was a bizarre experience. Catherine still felt she was suspended in midair, when in actuality she was now miles beneath the surface of the earth. They willed themselves to go deeper still.

Suddenly, from far beneath them there was light. Shining through the rock below came a fiery radiance. Magma. They'd almost reached the shoreless ocean of white-hot molten rock that made up the earth's core.

"I think we're deep enough," Lys said. "The rock around us now must be part of Iona's tectonic plate."

"How will we find the fault line?"

"I'm not sure, but I'm assuming there will be some visible indication of it."

They willed themselves to drift to the south, in the direction of the Isle of Islay. They knew the fault had to pass somewhere between Iona and Islay.

Gliding forward, they carefully scanned the rock ahead, searching for any trace of the plate boundary. At this depth, there was not much to see. While there were minor variations in the color and texture of the rock, they both felt they were entombed in a slowly shifting greyish-brown blur. The monotony was maddening.

With no visible landmarks, it was difficult to

judge their speed or the distance they'd covered, but Lys felt they must have already traveled several miles. *What if they'd gone past it? What if there were no visible signs of the plate boundary?*

Ten minutes later they saw it. From the shadow realm, it appeared they were approaching a dark wall of tortured stone, thousands of feet high, dozens of feet wide, and extending as far as they could see in either direction.

"This must be it," Lys said in amazement. "The fault line! Along this boundary, the tectonic plates are slowly grinding against each other, propelled by subtle currents in the magma below."

"The pressure here must be immense," Catherine said. "I can't imagine the forces that are acting on these plates."

"Friction between the plates usually prevents much movement, but occasionally the boundary softens enough for the plates to slip past each other. The result is an earthquake. As the plates here move, the land above them shifts, sometimes tearing sideways and sometimes rising dozens of feet into the air.

"Our goal is to soften the boundary between the plates and allow the surging magma below to force Iona upward."

Seeing the immensity of the boundary line before them, Catherine was taken aback. "Are you sure we can do this? I mean, this fault line must run for hundreds of miles. How can we begin to have an effect on it?"

"I'm not sure we can," Lys admitted. "It

would definitely be impossible for the two of us alone, but remember that we now have more than five hundred singers to help us.

"And these plates are not really connected. They're constantly grating against each other. They're *trying* to move. We just need to lubricate them a little.

"We'll position singers every five hundred feet along the boundary south of Iona and see what happens."

After returning to the surface, Lys called a meeting of the most experienced singers and prepared them to lead teams into the depths of the earth.

Chapter Thirty: Final Days

THE ISLAND OF IONA

The work on Stonehenge was progressing. Erin was pleased to discover that telekinesis made the work of quarrying, shaping and transporting the massive stones almost effortless. All of the replacement stones had arrived in Stonehenge seven days before the comet was scheduled to strike. Using their gift of telekinesis, the construction crew, guided by Michael Fletcher, began re-assembling the ancient portal.

The work of raising Iona was going less well. In fact, it did not appear to be working at all. Lys had shifts of one hundred singers each stationed deep in the earth along the junction of the tectonic plates. There appeared to be some softening in the boundary between the plates, but there was little indication of movement.

It was agreed that the singers would continue their effort to raise Iona until the impact of Wormwood Alpha. Once the first comet had struck, whether Iona had shifted or not, the singers would withdraw to Stonehenge and attempt to open the portal.

If all went according to plan, the singers should be able to open the Great Portal of the South at least ten hours before the Wormwood Beta struck. That would give them the window Patrick had hoped for. With a portal to Hades open, Patrick and Roger would lead rescue teams into Hades in an attempt to save as many captives as possible.

A call went out for volunteers for an invasion of Hell, and more than two-thousand newly restored men and women responded.

Erin scheduled the volunteers to meet with Roger in groups of fifty, to prepare them for the task ahead. The first group was scheduled to arrive on Iona at 9 AM Tuesday morning. Erin had directed them to meet Roger on an isolated beach at the north end of the island.

At 8:47, there was a flash of light as the first volunteer appeared, stepping through a rift from Glasgow. It was a young man, barely twenty years old and clearly excited that he had actually opened a rift and passed through it successfully. He glanced around to make sure he was in the right place.

As Roger greeted him, there were three more flashes of light in quick succession. Three more volunteers had arrived. A middle-aged woman from London, a younger woman from the Midlands, and a teenaged boy from Edinburgh.

Before Roger could even greet them, there were more flashes.

People had begun streaming through rifts from all over the British Isles, to the deserted beach at the north end of Iona.

They were a rag-tag group, men and women as young as 14 and as old as 70, but all had responded to the call to mount a rescue mission to the netherworld. Being synaxis members, a number of them recognized each other and were soon locked in conversation.

As the volunteers milled around talking, Roger activated his life force and rose twenty feet into the air. He appeared to be clothed in a brilliant golden light, with multicolored flames in constant motion across and around his body. The air around him crackled with energy. In his right hand, he held a sword that glistened with golden light.

Without saying a word, he aimed the sword at a rock formation fifty feet away. Something like ball lightning shot down the length of the sword and struck the rock, causing it to explode with an ear-piercing concussion.

Having gotten the attention of everyone present, Roger sheathed his sword, allowed his life force to fade, and stood facing the group at the top of a small rise of land overlooking the beach.

The assembled would-be warriors gazed at Roger in awe.

"What you have just seen is a demonstration of a power all of you now possess. When you first experienced transformation, we tried to train you in the basics: opening rifts, flying, entering the shadow realm. But you have other abilities you are not yet aware of. Your enhanced life force can be used as a weapon. We hope using that weapon will not often be necessary, but in this mission it is essential.

"Today I will be training you to fight as warriors in the oldest battle known to mankind. It's the battle of good against evil. All of you have been victims of that battle. You've all been oppressed by Archons in ways you never even suspected. You've all had friends and relatives who were casualties.

"But now you have a way to fight back.

"Since your restoration, you have all the power you need to overcome the enemy.

"Your restored life-force can be a fearsome weapon in this battle. Today I'm going to show you how to use it."

Roger explained the basics of using their new ability, then took time with each of them to make sure they were able to do it.

The entire training session took less than an hour, *which is good*, Roger thought wearily. It was a speech he'd have to repeat 39 more times over the next few days.

Three days before Wormwood Alpha struck, the Great Portal at Stonehenge was finally completed. There was no way to test it, since the singers were all still occupied at Iona, but in reality there was no need for testing. They had done all that they knew to do. Either it would work, or it would not. They would find out in three days.

Meanwhile, the attempt to raise Iona was going nowhere.

Patrick explained the situation to Michael and Erin at breakfast. "There are indications that the boundary between the tectonic plates has softened considerably, and slight movement has occurred. But it's not enough to the save the island. If you've noticed the shoreline lately, it appears that the tide has gone out far beyond its normal limits. What's really happened is that the Island of Iona has actually risen about ten feet. While that proves the theory, we simply don't have enough time to make it work. At the present rate, it would take months to raise Iona out of danger."

"What seems to be the problem?"

"The singers have softened the boundaries between the tectonic plates, but they just can't provide enough upward thrust to make Iona rise any faster."

"Do you think we need to evacuate the island?" Erin asked.

"I hate to say it," Patrick responded, "but I think that would be wise."

"By the way," Erin added. "What about your folks in Northern Ireland? Will they be okay?"

"I just talked to them last night. Ireland's a big place. They assure me that they are far enough inland that the tidal wave should not affect them. Unfortunately, that's not the case for us on a tiny island like Iona."

"I'll get started on the plans for evacuation. It appears that a lot of the locals have already fled the island."

"Let's not be hasty about this," Michael countered. "I just had a brainstorm!

"What is it, Michael?"

"If the problem is a lack of enough upward pressure to move the tectonic plate, perhaps we can increase that pressure."

"How can we do that?"

"With *movers!*" Michael beamed, "people with

telekinetic gifts. They *move* things.

"So far, in our efforts to raise Iona, we've only used singers. The singers have softened the plate boundaries, but their gift can't produce the kind of lift we need.

"But I just got back from Stonehenge. A few days ago I saw Marissa lift a 25 ton sarsen, float it nearly a quarter-mile across a field, and set it gently in place, all while exerting no apparent effort. Her gift is growing incredibly strong, as are many of those with telekinetic gifts. At this point we really have no idea what they are capable of.

"The High King said it's not good to be alone. We've seen strong evidence of that. Gifts are often more effective when combined. That's why our gifts have always been more powerful in synaxis than individually.

"What if we link people with the gift of telekinesis with the singers. Adding 'movers' to the process may be able to add the upward pressure we need."

"We only have two days." Erin said hesitantly. "We'll try it for one day, but if we don't see results, we'll need to start the evacuation."

Marissa had just returned from Stonehenge, along with several other movers. They were meeting in Martyr's Bay Pub to celebrate the completion of their task, when Marissa's cell phone rang.

"Marissa, this is Erin. How many people do we have with a recognized gift of telekinesis?"

"Just over three hundred."

"Good. Meet me in Iona House in thirty

minutes. I have another job for you."

Within hours, teams of "movers" had joined the singers deep in the earth at the boundary of the tectonic plates, exerting upward pressure on the plate that formed the foundation of Iona and most of Northern Scotland.

When the sun rose the next morning, the difference was dramatic. The tide at the Bay at the Back of the Ocean had gone out further than anyone had ever seen. At the end of a long sloping beach was now a sheer cliff, towering fifty feet above the crashing surf below. On the eastern side of the island, the Sound of Iona had shrunk to half its normal width. The ferry linking Iona and Mull now sat high and dry on its moorings.

"I'd estimate that Iona rose about 100 feet overnight." Michael observed. "That's great progress, but is it enough?"

Throughout the day, the island continued to rise. The ground beneath their feet seemed continually in motion, vibrating and shifting with the upward surge of the tectonic plate. At times the earth would shudder with a cluster of small earthquakes, some powerful enough to cause pictures to fall from walls. By evening, Iona was at least three hundred feet above its original level.

Wormwood Alpha was scheduled to strike in the mid-Atlantic about 4:00 PM the next day.

The movers had been working in shifts of four hours on and four hours off. It was decided to bring them all in at the same time.

The singers continued to work in shifts, singing only an hour at a time to protect their voices. Whether Iona was saved or not, the singers had to be able to open the Stonehenge portal the next day.

Positioned in the shadow realm, deep in the recesses of the earth, the singers continued their song, while those with the gift of telekinesis applied constant, upward pressure on Iona's tectonic plate. And slowly, ever-so-slowly, the earth moved.

Chapter Thirty-One: First Strike

THE ISLAND OF IONA, SCOTLAND

The impact of Wormwood Alpha was devastating. Smashing into the North Atlantic at 132,000 mph, it exploded with unprecedented fury.

The largest nuclear bomb ever exploded was the Tsar Bomb, detonated by the USSR in 1961. Its power was estimated to be 50 megatons. The explosion created by Wormwood Alpha was not 50 megatons, but 2 hundred million megatons.

The comet ripped through the atmosphere and plunged into the sea, instantly vaporizing billions of tons of sea water. In the coming hours, molten rock from the sea floor would rain down as far as 800 miles away. Plumes of superheated steam injected into the jet stream spawned super-hurricanes that pummeled the planet.

Perhaps worst of all, the cataclysm created a 600-foot-high mega-tsunami that moved outward in all directions.

But the efforts of the exhausted singers and movers had produced the desired effect. When the day of the impact dawned, the Bay at the Back of the Ocean stood atop a sheer cliff, 700 feet above the surface of the ocean.

They decided to continue their work until the

last minute, hopefully giving Iona an extra margin of safety.

When 3:45 came, everyone in the Iona synaxis stood atop a newly-formed, 900-foot cliff, waiting for the comet to strike.

At 4:07 pm, a brilliant flash of light brightened the eastern sky. Then nothing.

They all had the same thought. *Was it a dud?*

Sometime later, the shock wave hit. They watched it come sweeping across the surface of the Atlantic at the speed of sound. When it reached Iona, the island was engulfed in a thundering roar that seemed to shake the earth itself.

Then the sky in the distance gradually darkened. And finally it came. A wall of water unbelievably high was moving toward them. Even this far from the impact zone, the wave was massive. As it had spread outward, the wave had seemed to lose some of its power. But when it hit the continental shelf, it regained strength, increasing in height 'till it towered more than 500 feet above the surface of the sea.

"Surfs up!" Patrick muttered nervously as it came closer.

They all watched in terror as it approached. It seemed alive, an immense, lumbering monster — a living thing, crawling inexorably forward and devouring everything in its path.

It's rumored that the largest wave ever surfed was an astounding 108-foot mountain of water ridden by Benjamin Sanchis in Nazare, Portugal on December 11, 2015.

The wave approaching Iona now was at least five times that height.

As it drew near, everyone in the synaxis had the same question. *Had they succeeded in saving the island? Had what they accomplished been enough?*

Approaching the island, the wave seemed to increase in intensity, swelling ever higher. As a precaution, the synaxis members activated their life force and rose several hundred feet into the air. Even from that height, the wave was terrifying.

The distance between the wave and the island gradually narrowed.

And then it struck.

With a roar that shook the entire island, the incoming tsunami crashed against the newly formed escarpment. Enormous clouds of spray and spume exploded skyward, rising thousands of feet in the air and showering Iona with a salt-water rain. The heaving sea mounted almost to the top of the cliff, but then hesitated and fell back.

But another swell rose on its heels. The wave surged even higher, but it too could not overtop the cliff.

Then a final swell came, slamming the cliff face with an earth-shaking rumble, but it also fell back in defeat.

The monster wave had finally exhausted itself and began to slowly dissipate.

The island of Iona was saved, and the Iona portal preserved.

With the exhausted singers and movers no longer at their subterranean posts, the Island of Iona gradually began to subside.

The movers returned to their homes for a well-deserved rest. But the singers still had a job to do.

PART FOUR: RESCUE MISSION

Chapter Thirty-Two:
Into the Darkness

STONEHENGE – ON THE
SALISBURY PLAIN, UK

An army of 2000 restored humans had assembled on the broad plain around Stonehenge. The singers had arrived from Iona and were positioned just outside the sarsen circle, waiting for the signal to open the portal.

The sky to the west was already darkening as the hurricane spawned by Wormwood Alpha drew near, but the sky overhead remained clear. Wormwood Beta now seemed enormous, its shining tail stretching halfway across the sky, visible even in daylight hours. It was due to hit the earth in less than nine hours.

Roger had spent several days working with groups of restored humans, teaching them to use their life-force as a weapon, just as he had done in the sheik's torture chamber. While many of the volunteers were still clumsy and uncertain, they were totally committed, and their gifts were lethal.

Erin Fletcher hovered twenty feet in the air, where her voice could be heard by all. As always,

Erin exuded an aura of beauty. Her body was tall and well-proportioned, and her perfectly formed face was framed by rich cascades of silken, chestnut-brown hair. The golden glow of her life-force gave her the appearance of an angel.

As she began to speak, Erin instantly captured the attention of everyone present. "I want to thank all of you for volunteering for this task. I need to warn you that there is great danger in what you are about to do. Because of the restoration, your normal lifespan is now hundreds of thousands of years. You are no longer condemned to grow old and die in forty or fifty years, but you can still be destroyed. Some of you may not survive this mission.

"When you get to Abadon, you will find yourselves greatly outnumbered. Believing the earth is about to be destroyed, almost all of the Archons abandoned the Earth-realm days ago. That means all the demons who once infested our world are back in Hades, most of them in the city of Abadon. The influx of new Archons may well have doubled the city's population.

"When you encounter them, they will no longer be evil influences operating from the shadow realm. They'll be fully-armed warriors committed to your destruction.

"The good news is that we have the element of surprise. The Archons believe our world is about to end and won't be expecting a rescue attempt. But our advantage may not last long. At the most, it will give you time to get to the crater and start the evacuation.

"Once word spreads that you are trying to free

their captives, the Archon hordes will be on you very quickly.

"The Great Portal of Abadon is our only way in and out of Hades, but once you are in that realm, you can open a rift to any other location, just as you do on earth.

"Since Lys, Roger, and Michael know the route through the city, they will lead the initial invasion, guiding you down the corridors of Abadon to the ancient crater where the majority of the slaves are imprisoned. Along the way you will attempt to dispatch any Archons you encounter while gathering as many slaves as possible.

"From Patrick's dreams, we think we have a good idea what we'll find when we get to the crater. While Patrick and the first 1000 warriors try to hold the banshees at bay, Jamie and Michael will open rifts from the crater back to the portal of Abadon and attempt to lead the captives out.

"While the slaves are exiting the crater, Roger, Lys and Marissa will lead a second force of 1000 warriors to the arena. At the arena, Roger and the human warriors will run interference with the Archons, while Lys and Marissa release the prisoners from their bonds and herd them into a rift.

"We believe this plan will allow us to rescue the maximum number of slaves, but it's all contingent on how the Archons respond.

"If at any point you are overwhelmed by the Archon forces, you *must* get out immediately. We don't have time for a prolonged battle. We may not be able to free all the captives, but we'll do what we can.

"We want to give ourselves a margin of error, so your time limit is seven hours. In seven hours, every one of you *must* be back in the Earth-realm."

The singers were positioned around the great sarsen circle. Only a small fraction of the singers would be used during the rescue attempt, and they would operate in shifts, keeping the portal continually open.

When the time came for Wormwood Beta to strike, the rest of the singers would join in, attempting to extend the portal to its greatest possible dimensions.

When all was in place, Patrick, Michael, Lys and Roger stood with Jamie and Marissa before the great trilithon in the center of Stonehenge. Thousands of warriors stood ready to follow them into the portal, when it opened.

"I can't help thinking about the last time we went into Abadon," Lys said with shudder as she looked at the circle of stones around them. "I hoped I'd never see that place again."

"I vowed I'd rather die than go back," Jamie said, as images of the tortures she'd endured flashed in her mind. "There's a huge part of me that does *not* want to do this!"

"This time will be different," Michael countered. "The Archons have plundered and oppressed us for thousands of years. Now it's our turn to plunder them."

For Marissa and Patrick, this would be their first times to experience Hades, though Marissa's time in the sheikh's playroom had given her a taste of what the place was like. Patrick's experience had only been through his dreams, but in many ways his memories were just as vivid as the rest. They all tried to steel themselves for what lay ahead.

At a word from Michael, the singers began to sing.

Positioned around the outer circle of sarsen stones, the singers began quietly; in fact, their song was barely discernable. Michael had to look to be sure they had actually begun. The massive stones of Stonehenge seemed to be capturing the sound.

As they continued, however, the voices grew louder and more powerful. The ancient structure seemed to resonate to the singer's voices.

Then suddenly, Stonehenge began to shake. The multi-ton lintels of the great sarsen circle trembled and rocked with greater and greater intensity.

Michael was alarmed. *Was something wrong? Was there some aspect of the construction they had overlooked?*

The shaking increased. The massive stones were visibly quaking. Seven-ton lintels seemed to be bouncing almost an inch into the air. Michael was tempted to stop the singers, but he knew of no other alternative. The portal *must* be opened now. Yet as the shaking continued, his distress was visible. *Will it all fall down?*

As the singing continued, however, the shaking gradually subsided. A rushing wind began to blow, turning the interior of the structure into a whirlwind, and then from the earth beneath Stonehenge, a beam of light shot skyward.

For the first time in thousands of years, the Great Portal at Stonehenge had opened. As the light intensified, the six humans standing in the center of the circle simply disappeared.

They had the sensation of falling. ...a long, slow fall into darkness. Then, suddenly there was solid ground beneath their feet. Looking around, they saw that they were now standing in Hades, just outside the city of Abadon.

The six believed their plan to be simple, well thought-through, and foolproof. They would move quickly, rescue all the hostages they could, and be out of Hades before the comet struck.

But of course, things rarely go according to plan.

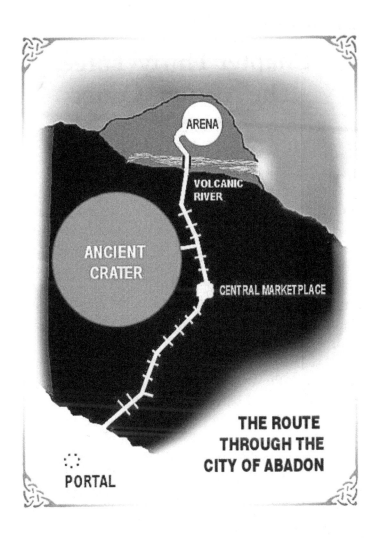

ARENA

VOLCANIC RIVER

ANCIENT CRATER

CENTRAL MARKET PLACE

THE ROUTE
THROUGH THE
CITY OF ABADON

PORTAL

Chapter Thirty-Three: The Ancient Crater

THE CITY OF ABADON, HADES

As they felt solid ground beneath their feet, the team glanced around, trying to orient themselves. They found themselves in the center of a large circle of standing stones.

A barren wasteland stretched to the horizon under a dark, overcast sky that slowly pulsed with dull, red light. Clouds of yellow, sulfurous dust scudded across the desolate plain. The place was oppressively hot.

Far to the right stood the crumbling ruins of a large city—the original city of Abadon. Before the great wars, it had been a metropolis of shining, cloud-piercing towers. Now only jagged skeletons of dark, twisted steel stood vigil above the lifeless plain.

Immediately behind them, a jagged mountain rose abruptly—the front range of more dark peaks beyond. Several volcanos were erupting in the distance, spewing clouds of ash mixed with glowing cinders into the already darkened sky.

"Welcome back to Hades," Lys muttered, taking a deep breath.

On a cliff face, just 300 feet away, yawned the gaping maw of an immense cavern. The entrance had the shape of a human mouth frozen in a scream of anguish. Jamie shuddered at the sight.

"What *is* that?" Marissa asked, pointing toward the cavern.

"That, my dear, is the gate of Hell," Michael said glumly. "In Dante's poem, the gateway to Hell bore a terrifying inscription, 'Abandon hope, all ye who enter here.'

"The entrance to Abadon lacks an inscription, but Dante's words would certainly apply. Millions of human captives have passed through that cavern entrance, but only a handful have escaped alive.

"And that handful of survivors are standing beside you right now," Jamie added. "I only hope we're as fortunate in making our escape this time."

"The captives in there have already abandoned hope," Patrick interjected. "I've seen them in my dreams every night for weeks now. They've resigned themselves to an existence of torture and slavery. But we're here the change that."

Seeing the trepidation on Jamie's face, he added, "The Archons are not expecting an army of restored humans, Jamie. Most of them have never *seen* a restored human. They have no idea what's about to hit them."

"I know you're right," Jamie responded. "But I still dread the thought of going back in there."

As the six moved out of the stone circle, groups of human warriors began to appear behind them. They poured through in a continuous stream until an army of some 2000 men and women stood behind them on the sulfurous plain.

Following Roger's lead, the human warriors all

activated their life-force. The impression was breath-taking. Each warrior suddenly shown with a brilliant golden glow while multicolored flames danced around and across their bodies.

Rising several feet above the ground, the warriors drew their swords and followed Roger as he led the way toward the entrance of Abadon. Viewed together, they appeared to be a river of light flowing across the desolate plain. As they approached the city, the shining river poured through the gaping cavern entrance, then flowed down into darkness.

The mouth of the cavern was immense, arching several hundred feet above them. The warriors descended into the depths of the mountain through a wasteland of black, twisted volcanic rock. Moving onward, the light from the surface grew dim, until all they saw was a dim, red glow that seemed to emanate from the rocks themselves.

As they continued to glide silently forward, the natural cavern transitioned into a tunnel burrowed deep into the mountain. While not as large as the cavern entrance, the tunnel was still immense, 40 feet wide and at least 60 feet high. Many smaller side tunnels branched from the main one.

Lys, Michael and Roger vividly remembered the route. Alert to possible dangers, they led the warriors onward.

The place was deserted.

Following the main corridor through the city, they peered down every side passage but saw no one. There were no slaves and no Archons.

"What's happened here?" Lys asked. "I thought

the city would be crowded and bustling with activity, but it looks like it's been abandoned."

"With their mental powers, they may have anticipated our coming and staged an ambush," Roger replied. "Be on your guard."

As they approached the center of the city, the passageway widened and the ceiling arched more than 100 feet above their heads.

For the 2000 warriors, this was their first time to experience Hades. As they advanced along the corridor, they glanced around, open mouthed, awestruck at the sheer size of the place.

Looking up, Lys saw one of the city's great vertical shafts. It was at least forty feet wide and seemed to stretch upward into infinity. It was a passageway into the upper levels of the city. On their previous visit, Lys remembered that these shafts had been alive with Archons, darting blurs, swerving and twisting. A continuous cacophony of hideous screeches had echoed down from the cavernous chambers above. Now all was silent.

They moved on, staying alert to sudden attack, certain that a fierce horde of Archons would appear at any moment. But it never happened.

"We're almost to the central marketplace," Roger warned. "It's one of the busiest places in Abadon—lots of slaves and lots of Archons. We're almost certain to encounter some resistance there. Be ready."

The corridor before them enlarged into a huge gallery that obviously had once been a great magma dome. The roof soared three hundred feet above a broad plaza.

"This is the central marketplace," Roger said, glancing around. He allowed his life-force to fade, planting his feet on the ground as he set out to explore. The rest followed his example, holding their swords at the ready.

"Where *is* everybody?" Lys asked again.

Along the sides of the great magma dome were markets and shops. Storefronts were also carved into the gallery wall six or seven stories high, many accessible only to flying Archons, or to slaves terrified enough of their masters to brave the precarious narrow stairways carved into the cliff face.

They peered into each shop they passed, but the shops were all closed and the plaza deserted. Their footsteps echoed as they walked.

At the far side of the plaza, they encountered their first slave. The man cowered before them, trembling violently in fear. As they approached, he let out an anguished scream and fled down a side passage.

"What's going on here?" Lys asked again, remembering what the marketplace had been like when she'd last seen it. "Where did everybody go?"

"Could they have discovered our plan and fled to a different dimension?"

Patrick glanced at his watch. "We don't have long to find out. It's now six hours to comet strike. Erin wants us to be out of here in five."

Activating their life-force again, they exited the

marketplace and continued down the main corridor in the direction of the arena, until they came to a wide corridor that branched to the left.

Gliding two-hundred yards down the side corridor brought them out onto a balcony three hundred feet above an immense, circular field that stretched before them for more than half a mile. It had once been the central crater of the ancient volcano. Over the centuries, its yawning pit had been filled in by tailings as the underground city was excavated, producing a broad, gravel-covered plain.

The last time Roger, Lys and Michael had been here, the place had been a training ground for Archon warriors. It was obvious that it had been repurposed.

The walls of the crater formed immense cliffs that surrounded the field on every side, rising upward for thousands of feet. The pit was open to the elements, and illuminated by the dull light of Hades' perpetually overcast sky. It was now a place of unimaginable horror.

The crater was everything Patrick had seen in his dreams and more.

It looked like every slave in Abadon had now been crammed into the crater. A pall of depression hung over them. The captives sat, motionless, many weeping, many sobbing or wailing in uncontrolled anguish. Along one end of the crater floor were row after row of breeding pens, thousands of them, filled with battered, bruised, and helpless women — the breeding stock of the Archon's new humanity. Stripped naked, caged, and subjected to daily sexual assault, many of the women were too overwhelmed with shame to even raise their eyes. The place was filthy. The stench of unwashed bodies, along with untreated sewage, was overpowering.

No Archons were visible anywhere.

Over their heads, in the middle of the crater, was a huge, holographic projection displaying the recent destruction of Earth's cities.

Evidently, the last Archons to leave the Earth-realm had made a recording of the impact of Wormwood Alpha. That depiction now played in a continuous loop before the horrified eyes of the captives. The loop began with a shot of Alpha impacting the earth. The Archons had recorded the resulting explosion from several angles, along with the tidal wave spreading outward. Then came views of individual cities.

First, they witnessed the death of New York City. The warriors watched in horror as the tidal wave thundered across Lower New York Bay. Surging through the narrows between Staten Island and Brooklyn, it constricted and increased in height. As tall as a sixty-story building, the wave crossed Upper New York Bay, toppling the Statue of Liberty in an instant. Ellis Island was erased. Jersey City obliterated.

Then it struck Manhattan Island. Coming ashore at Battery Park, the monster crawled inexorably up the island, tall buildings toppling before it like pins before a bowling ball. Wall Street and the financial district were gone in a moment. Soho, Greenwich Village, and the

Theater District were swept away. The Empire State Building stood proudly against the flood for almost two seconds before it also crumbled.

When New York City finally lay in watery ruins, the projection shifted to Boston. City after city followed, leaving the impression that all of human civilization had been destroyed.

And all the while, at the bottom of the screen, a countdown timer ticked off the seconds until Wormwood Beta struck, obliterating what was left of planet earth.

The Archons had arranged that every slave in Abadon would witness their world's destruction. In some ways, this was the worst Archon torture of all. It robbed the slaves of their last microscopic vestige of hope.

No matter how bad things had been in Hades, the captives had all secretly clung to the knowledge that the world they had known was still there, that their loved ones still lived, and that somehow, some day, they might be able to escape and return.

Now that hope was crushed. There was nothing to return to. Their world was gone, leaving them isolated and abandoned.

Motioning for the warriors to remain on the balcony, Roger flew to the crater floor followed by Jamie, Patrick, Lys, Marissa, and Michael. Standing on a rise of land at the edge of the crater, Roger attempted to gain the attention of the captives.

"Listen to me!" he shouted. "We're here to rescue you! We've come to take you out of this place."

No one moved. Few even looked up.

Puzzled by the lack of response, Roger called out to Michael, Lys, and Marissa to open rifts.

Drawing their swords the three humans lifted them over their heads and brought them down in a swift stroke. With a sound like the rumble of distant thunder, the air parted, creating rifts in the atmosphere—ragged, brilliantly-glowing ribbons of energy surrounding tunnels of total darkness. The three rifts hung suspended in mid-air, each forming a passage leading directly to the Great Portal of Abadon.

But the rifts drew little response from the captive crowd.

Roger shouted again, "Come with us! We'll take you back to your own world."

Stunned by the blank looks of the few who bothered to look at all, Roger shouted again, "What you see here are rifts. I know you've never seen them before, but they're your means of escape. Stepping into one of these rifts will transport you instantly to the Great Portal of Abadon. That portal is now open. You can escape this place! Just walk through any one of these rifts and proceed to the stone circle. You'll be back in the Earth-realm within minutes!"

Still no one responded.

Finally, someone called out in hopeless desperation. "There's no place to go back to! Our homes and families are destroyed. The Archons showed us what happened when the first comet struck. There's not much left now... And anything that *is* left will be gone in a few hours."

"What you saw in that recording is true, but it

is not the whole story. A small comet did impact the earth. There was great destruction along the Atlantic coast, but most of the people were evacuated. The Earth is still there.

"It's true that a second comet is coming, a much larger one. But it will not destroy the earth. It will destroy Hades. That's why you must leave here now!"

As Roger was speaking, Grat Dalton entered the crater through a side tunnel. Seeing Roger and the others addressing the captives, he walked briskly in their direction;

Glaring at the six in disbelief, he spat, "If it isn't the damn synaxis! You people don't know when to quit, do you?"

Recognizing Jamie, his lips tightened in a cruel grin. "And there's my old friend Jamie Thatcher. We had so much fun together at Raven's Nest, I guess you've come back for another helping."

Jamie's mind filled with pictures of the harrowing night spent in the tunnels of Carrington's underground fortress. She remembered finding Nicole brutally murdered — her body lying in a pool of blood with her throat slashed from ear to ear by Grat Dalton.

Then Jamie was fleeing from Grat. He pursued her relentlessly through narrow tunnels in total darkness, his 16-inch Bowie knife in hand, determined to rip the life from her defenseless body.

"We have lots of dark tunnels here, Jamie." Grat smirked, retrieving his razor-sharp blade from its sheath in his right boot. "How about a rematch?"

Roger stepped forward to defend his wife, but Jamie cut in front of him. "Leave him to me!"

"It's been a long time Dalton!" she spat.

"You thought you were in control in Raven's Nest. You thought you knew what was about to happen, but you were wrong. And you are just as wrong now. In five hours, this place, along with all the Archons, will be destroyed."

"That's a lie, Jamie, and you know it," Grat cut her off. "The Archons have already devastated your world and it's about to be destroyed. I've seen the pictures. These people are better off here. At least they're alive."

Taking a few steps closer, he continued, "You escaped from me in Raven's Nest, but that won't happen again," he drawled, casually pressing a stud on the communicator on his belt.

In response to Grat's call, a group of more than thirty banshees tore into the crater from a side tunnel, flying at high speed, darting and weaving. They were literal monsters, with a wingspan of over twenty feet, and lean, muscular bodies covered in gleaming black reptilian scales. Sinuous barbed tails lashed from side to side as they flew.

The banshees circled the crater, screeching loudly.

"I'm trying to decide," Grad said, taking another step closer. "Should I kill you quickly, or add you to my collection?"

His colorless lips stretched wide in a sadistic grin as he gestured toward the rows of crude, wire-pen cages lining the end of the crater. The appalling sight seared itself in Jamie's memory: row after row of wire cages held cringing, hollow-eyed women—their bruised, naked bodies coated with grime and filth. Jamie fought the urge to vomit.

"As you can see, my boys and me have a lot of fun here. This first row is all mine." He gloated. "But number four just got pregnant. She'll be out of circulation for a while. I'll need a replacement."

He eyed Jamie's slender form for a moment and smirked. "Looking at your body, Jamie, I think I might just keep you alive for a while. You'll be a fine addition to my breeding pens. Killing you quickly would be a tragic waste of female flesh!"

Having circled the crater, the banshees finally came to rest behind Grat. The lead monster's piercing green eyes were fixed on the humans, anticipating a kill. Her jaws spread wide, revealing a double set of long, jagged teeth.

"I warn you Grat; you and your pets better back off and let these people go! I've learned a few things since Raven's Nest. I'm not helpless anymore." She drew her sword, which instantly began to glow with a golden light.

But Grat had never encountered a restored human before and had no clue what power Jamie possessed.

Buoyed by the presence of the banshees, he sneered. "I'm not impressed by your tricks, Jamie, and I don't believe your lies." He advanced on Jamie, blade drawn, the banshees right behind him, shrieking and wailing.

But then, at a signal from Jamie, the two

thousand human warriors on the balcony above drew their swords, activated their life-force, and poured over the edge of the balcony in a glowing river—a three-hundred foot tall Niagara of brilliantly shining warriors, pouring into the ancient crater. In an instant, the warriors swarmed the banshees, killing several outright, and continuing to fire on them as they screeched and fled in terror. Not a banshee escaped.

Seeing his banshees in retreat, a look of horror crossed Grat's face. He turned to leave, but warriors had landed all around him. His escape was cut off.

Jamie had no doubt that Grat would have killed her without mercy, or even worse, enslaved her in his pens as he had so many other women. But just killing him seemed too easy.

Looking at the women caged in Grat's breeding pens, Jamie had an idea. "Seize him!" Several human warriors moved to disarm and immobilize Grat Dalton.

"Now, get those women out of the pens and lead them through the rifts."

As Grat watched, his cringing captives were released and led trembling through the rifts to freedom.

"Dalton, I'm not going to kill you. I'm going to let the comet do that. But until that happens, I'm going to give you a taste of the humiliation you've inflicted on those women. Your last hours of life will be spent crouched in a filthy breeding pen watching your captives escape to freedom.

"Strip him naked!" Jamie ordered, "and lock

him in the smallest pen you can find. And make sure it's secure."

Grat struggled against his captors with every fiber of his being, but it was to no avail. While other warriors held him down, one of the largest seized Grat's razor-sharp knife and used it to strip the clothing from his body. Grat soon found himself bruised, naked and vulnerable, caged in a three-foot by five-foot wire pen. His former victims gazed at him in incredulity.

Grat glared at Jamie with unmitigated rage. "Wait till the Archons get back, *bitch*," he hissed. "We'll see who's in a cage then."

Ignoring him, Jamie turned and again called to the captives. "Do you see this! Dalton's in a cage and the banshees are dead! There's nothing left to hold you. You're free to leave!"

There was still no movement.

"This place is about to be destroyed!" She screamed, "You have to leave *now!*"

Encouraged by the sight of the dead banshees, a few brave stragglers responded. They rose and limped toward the closest rift. As they disappeared into it, others rose to follow. Many more rifts were opened, and soon thousands at a time were streaming out of the crater.

A good number of the captives chose to detour past Grat's pen as they left. Some looked at him in disgust and shook their heads, but others cursed him loudly. Many spat on him. One large man crouched down, face-to-face with Dalton, and spewed a stream of unrepeatable profanities. Having apparently run out of expletives, the man straightened up and turned to leave, but then turned back. The man glared down at his former captor for a moment longer, then in a show of utter contempt, he lifted the front of his slave smock and urinated on Grat Dalton. Soon dozens of men had lined up to follow his example.

Jamie decided to allow the captives freedom to vent their rage. After what they'd all suffered at Grat's hand, she felt they had the right. And Grat certainly deserved whatever he got.

Even with many rifts open, it still took hours for the massive tide of humanity to flow through the rifts and into the portal. The warriors hovered overhead, keeping watch. And all the while the question remained, "Where are the Archons?"

With barely two hours left before the comet strike, Roger looked at Lys, "I think things here are under control. It's time to get to the arena."

Nachash, the Archon
Sacred Mountain

Chapter Thirty-Four: The Arena Revisited

THE ARENA – CITY OF ABADON

Leaving half of the warriors to keep watch at the crater, an army of shining warriors, 1000 strong, flowed back to the main corridor of the city and made their way toward the arena.

The path leaving the city wound upward between enormous, convoluted blocks of hardened lava. Finally exiting the city of Abadon, they saw before them, silhouetted dark against the overcast sky, an immense dragon, its angular head raised high on a serpentine neck, eyes fixed in their direction.

The dragon was not alone. Twenty feet to the left stood a hideous, nine-headed monster. Behind the dragon and the monster were two rows of other repugnant beasts: harpies, manticores, gorgons, gryphons, chimeras and hydras. They all stood in silence, unmoving.

The restored humans knew exactly what they were seeing. The path ahead led between two rows of enormous gargoyles, adorning an ancient bridge that arched above a deep canyon. A twelve-foot tall stone dragon and an equally tall nine-headed monster stood as sentinels at the entrance to the bridge. The smaller beasts, still nine feet tall, were arrayed on either side of a broad walkway that ran down the center of the bridge. Two more twelve-foot tall gargoyles, a basilisk and a Minotaur, served as sentinels on the far end.

Lys now understood the significance of the beasts. The gargoyles depicted the artificial life forms created by the Archons to lead the first attack on the Earth-realm. She pictured in her mind millions of these monsters swarming the great cities of ancient earth.

Lys led the way as the warriors crossed the bridge, then flowed down a gradual slope, winding through a wasteland of black, twisted, rock — the remains of an ancient lava flow. The stench of burning sulfur was heavier here and breathing was becoming difficult. Exiting the lava flow, they found themselves on a broad, paved esplanade overlooking the arena.

The panorama before them was horrifying. Jagged volcanic peaks surrounded them on three sides, with more volcanos in the distance. From the erupting volcanos, columns of smoke mixed with glowing ash billowed skyward. White-hot lava gushed from several peaks, pouring down the mountainsides in rivers of liquid fire, then cascading in blazing torrents to a sea of molten lava in the valley below.

Below them, quarried into the surface of a broad plateau, situated high above the fiery sea, was the arena, a vast bowl-like depression, a quarter-mile across, illuminated by the surrounding volcanic fires. Its interior was terraced, forming nine concentric rings. They'd all heard the reports of what took place there.

The arena was a real-life Dante's Inferno—a pit where humans were subjected to unspeakable torments for the entertainment of their Archon captors. At each descending level, the severity of the tortures increased. On the top level, punishments were painful but did not inflict lasting damage. At lower levels, however, slaves were mutilated in ever more grotesque ways. The lowest level was a place for extreme torture and execution.

Lys flew to the edge of the esplanade and gazed out across the arena.

Above the roar of the volcanos, the arena usually reverberated with an unceasing cacophony of human shrieks, howls, agonized screams, and pleas for mercy. Today the scene was much more subdued. Less than half the usual number of slaves were present. No Archons were visible, yet torture still continued, inflicted at the hands of human guards.

Most of the victims looked like they had been in their place of torture for a number of hours. Some were already dead. Lys got the impression that in the midst of torturing their captives, the Archons had been suddenly called away, and simply left the arena.

Where did the Archons go?

On the top level of the arena, Marissa found a large, solidly-built man crammed into a tiny steel cage. His body was locked in a fetal position with his chin forced against his chest and arms and legs pressed tightly against the bars, leaving him unable to move and barely able to breathe. He had obviously been confined in that position for a number of hours.

He was whimpering with pain, barely conscious.

While Lys and the warriors spread out across the arena to release other captives, Marissa quickly found the latch to release the man and eased his body from the cage. Each of his limbs, held immobile for hours, seemed frozen in place. It was only with great pain that the man forced himself to move. Every movement brought terrible anguish.

Filled with compassion, Marissa gently massaged his cramped muscles, helping to restore circulation.

As his pain began to diminish, Marissa asked, "Can you tell us what happened here? Where have the Archons gone?"

"They've gone to Nachash, their sacred mountain," he said, lifting a trembling finger in the direction of the distant volcanos.

"They're having a celebration," he continued. "It's their day of victory. The human race has finally been defeated. The Earth-realm will be destroyed today."

Beyond the line of nearby volcanos belching columns of smoke mixed with glowing ash, Marissa could just make out the dim form of a much larger mountain in the distance. Given the apparent distance, it must have been many times the size of the nearer volcanos. The top of the mountain seemed to be surrounded in haze. Then Marissa realized to her horror that the apparent haze was actually a cloud made up of millions upon millions of Archons swarming around the volcano's peak. Almost the entire Archon race had gathered for a great celebration.

"They've taken 1000 human slaves with them," the man added. "Newly harvested slaves from the Earth-realm. At the exact moment the earth is destroyed, they'll fling the slaves alive into the lake of fire at the volcano's heart to commemorate the end of human resistance."

As the man spoke, he began to weep, anguished tears pouring down his cheeks. While his pain was gradually decreasing, he was overcome with grief. He shared the utter hopelessness of the captives in the ancient crater.

"But that's not correct," Marissa assured him. "The Earth-realm is not going to be destroyed. That was the Archon's plan, but it's been foiled. The earth will continue. In fact, the Archon plan has backfired. It's Hades that will be destroyed. We've come here to rescue you before that happens."

While the warriors drove back the human guards, slaves who had been set free from their bonds were slowly making their way to the top of the arena.

Marissa raised her glowing sword and opened a rift to the Great Portal. Slowly, the tortured humans began to hobble toward it.

Looking up, a chill traveled down Marissa's spine as she saw one of the human guards standing on the edge of the esplanade speaking into a communicator.

Within minutes, there was a visible change on the distant mountain. Hearing the news of the rescue attempt, the Archon hordes broke off their celebration and rose as one, heading back to Abadon to confront the intruders.

"We've got the get these people out of here *quickly!*" Marissa screamed. "Every demon in Hell is headed this way!"

As Marissa continued to hold the rift open, Lys's eyes were fixed on the distant mountain. Marissa was right. The Archons had left the sacred mountain and were moving in their direction.

"I've got to go over there," Lys said. "There are a thousand human slaves on that mountain about to be executed."

Turning to Marissa she said, "Get the rest of these people to the portal. Judging by the distance to the sacred mountain, you shouldn't have any trouble getting them out before the Archons arrive.

"I'll rescue the slaves from the mountain and meet you back in the Earth-realm."

Roger glanced at his watch. "We need to be out of here in less than an hour, Sis. You don't have much time."

"I'll be careful!" Lys said, as she raised her sword to open a rift.

Roger hesitated a moment, then shouted, "I'm coming with you!"

He beckoned to some of the human warriors standing watch over the arena, and a half-dozen broke away to follow him to the sacred mountain

Meanwhile, Marissa stood at the rift she'd opened to the Great Portal of Abadon, calling the slaves to freedom. The restored human warriors hovered overhead, keeping the guards at bay.

At first, very few of the slaves were willing to

enter the rift. Most shrunk back in fear, seeming to choose the familiarity of torture in Hades over the frightening prospect of entering the unknown.

But slowly, gradually, they began to come. All were injured, some bleeding, some barely able to walk, but they came, and their numbers gradually increased, until they literally poured through the rift, anxious to escape the arena.

One man caught Marissa's attention. It was the man she'd released from the cramped cage. Though obviously still in great pain himself, he didn't rush into the rift as many were now doing. Instead, he was finding those too weak or too injured to walk, carrying them up the ramps to the rift, then returning to find someone else. Over and over he did it, pushing himself to the limits of his strength. When there was no one else to help, he finally came up to the rift himself.

As he hobbled to the edge of the rift, he glanced up at Marissa and said two words. They were simple words, but words none of the other captives had thought to say. The man looked Marissa in the eye, and with tears streaming down his face said, "Thank you!"

Marissa smiled at him. "What's your name?"

"Clive," he said, wiping the sweat from his forehead before looking up again to meet her gaze. "Clive Stephens, from Glasgow, mum," he answered in a rich Scottish brogue.

"You're a good man, Clive Stephens from Glasgow. Now get through the rift. It's time to leave."

Marissa held the rift open as long as she dared, hoping others might still find their way. The Archon horde was drawing near. She was just about to close the rift when she saw one more man running up the ramp in her direction. He was a large man, and somehow familiar. It was immediately clear that he was not one of the tortured slaves. He was dressed in the black robe of an arena master, those charged by the Archons with doling out unspeakable punishments to the human slaves.

And then she saw his hideously deformed face.

It was the sheikh.

Rather than face punishment on earth, the sheikh had begged Kareina to take him to Hades, and she had agreed. She'd put him in charge of one of the lowest levels of the arena where he'd been able to satisfy his appetite for cruelty by inflicting terrible anguish on the doomed captives. It was a job well-suited to his skills.

Drawing close to the rift, the sheikh saw for the first time that the glowing being standing in front of it was Marissa. He stopped for a moment, alarmed.

Finally he spoke. "Marissa... my lovely *pet!*" He smiled nervously. "I'm so glad to see you looking so well. I heard what you said... that this world is about to be destroyed. You can't leave me here to die!" Tears were running down his malformed cheeks as he pleaded. "Please, my pet." His twisted mouth trembled in terror as he blubbered the words, "My sweet pet.

"I want you to know that of all of my

playthings, you were always my favorite. So beautiful. So strong. I beg you, let me go through that rift. I'll do anything you ask."

Marissa stared at him coldly for a moment.

She remembered the first time she'd glimpsed his deformed face and sensed the monstrous evil it concealed. She remembered the unspeakable pain she'd suffered at his hand.

But she now understood that the sheikh had been a victim of the Archons also. It had been the Archons who killed his family and deformed his face. The Archons had shaped his life, fashioning him as a tool to carry out their evil schemes. For an instant, Marissa actually felt a twinge of compassion for the man.

Yet the sheikh had willingly gone along with the Archon's plan. He had *chosen* to do what he did. She wondered how many pleas for mercy from his helpless victims the sheikh had spurned over the years.

She glanced around the nearly deserted arena and thought of the horrors that had taken place there. The sheikh was now part of this place. He had enthusiastically joined in its torments. This was truly *his* place, and it was truly where he deserved to die.

Marissa glared at him for what seemed like an eternity.

"My first inclination, *wahshan*, is to tell you to go to Hell..."

Marissa paused, looking one last time at the sheikh's hideously deformed countenance. The sheikh no longer looked ominous. He looked pathetic.

He continued to gaze up at her with pleading eyes, his whimpering lips still begging for mercy.

Finally, she said, "I would tell you to go to Hell, *wahshan*, but you're already *in* Hell, and it's truly where you belong.

"So I'll just leave you where you are."

And with that she stepped into the rift and allowed it to close.

Chapter Thirty-Five:
At the Sacred Mountain

NACHASH, THE ARCHON'S SACRED MOUNTAIN – HADES

As the cloud of Archons flew toward the arena, Lys opened a rift to Nachash, the Archon's sacred mountain. There, on a broad plateau just above the volcano's great rumbling mouth, a thousand human slaves were cowering in fear. They were men, women, and children of every race and ethnic group. All had been stripped naked for maximum humiliation. But they were not left unguarded.

Standing watch over the slaves were several dozen Archon warriors. Each of the monsters stood more than eight feet tall, ferocious and bestial in form. Their jaws hung open in a vicious grin and their green reptilian eyes shone with cold malevolence.

Behind them, great billows of smoke rose from the volcano's pit, glowing fiery red with glittering sparks rising high into the sky. Other erupting volcanos surrounded them on every side. At the edge of the pit stood two immense dragons.

Standing in front of the warriors and dragons, Lys was startled to see a familiar face. As their eyes met, her mouth fell open and her blood ran cold.

For as Lys and Roger stepped through the rift

onto the peak of Mount Nachash, Lys found herself face to face with Kareina Procel.

The dragons swung their long, sinuous necks toward the new arrivals, then one of them lifted its head high, and with a roar that shook the ground, belched a thick plume of flame and smoke high into the air.

Roger immediately went for the dragons. "I've got a score to settle here, Lys," he said. Drawing his sword he energized his life-force and rose into the air.

Seeing Roger moving in their direction, both beasts raised their leathery wings toward the sky and thrust them downward in a powerful stroke that lofted their bodies into the air. Another stroke lifted them higher and drove them forward with startling speed. Rising almost as one, the dragons traced a circle around the volcano's crater, then wheeled and headed directly toward Roger.

The larger of the two dragons was on Roger first.

Roger did not hesitate. He drove directly toward the dragon, extended his sword, and unleashed a bolt of energy.

But the dragon sideslipped and countered with a roar of dragonfire, narrowly missing Roger. Angling its wings to catch the searing updraft from the volcano's pit, the dragon rose high into the air with Roger in close pursuit.

Meanwhile, as the Archon guards closed in, the human warriors swarmed against them, leaving Lys to confront Kareina alone.

Lys was face-to-face with her oldest enemy.

Kareina stood for a moment studying her, then slowly drew her sword and began walking with grim determination in her direction.

A flood of cold, unreasoning fear crept up Lys's spine. Her lips silently formed two words. "O *shit!*"

Kareina's eyes narrowed to glowing coals and her mouth opened in anticipation as she moved closer.

Lys instinctively shrunk back. *This is it,* she thought. *It ends here. Only one of us will leave this mountain alive!*

"My old friend Lys," Kareina hissed. "Thank you so much for coming. What a perfect way for it all to end. Your world is about to be destroyed. And today I will destroy *you.*"

Lys's mind flashed with pictures of her previous encounters with Kareina

She remembered the harrowing chase down the twisting mountain roads of Colorado.

She saw again the hospital window, shattered by a gunshot that narrowly missed her and almost killed her brother.

She shuddered as she remembered the weeks-long assault by the shades that nearly drove her to suicide.

She saw herself being drugged and nearly drowned in the frigid waters of a Scottish loch.

As memory after memory flooded Lys's mind, her breath caught in her throat and an icy knot formed in her belly. Her hands were beginning to tremble. She continued to back away from Kareina.

Lys relived the terror she'd experienced at the base of Cnoc Nan Carnan when Kareina held a twelve-inch-long obsidian blade to her throat, raising it until its razor-sharp tip indented the soft flesh of her neck. Death had been moments away when Araton intervened.

Lys remembered being kidnapped the week before her wedding. She saw Kareina plunging the hypodermic into her thigh and remembered waking up naked on the concrete floor of the sheikh's torture chamber.

And now Kareina was here again. Lys knew that Kareina was determined not to fail this time.

Grinning malevolently, Kareina pressed in.

Consumed by raw terror, Lys's continued her retreat. Her heart was pounding, adrenaline flooding her blood stream. Lys gripped her sword with whitened knuckles.

Lys was almost to the rim of the crater. The intense heat radiating from the bubbling lava below scorched her flesh. Wisps of her light, ash-blonde hair were beginning to crackle and burn.

Roger had dispatched one dragon and was turning to the other when he saw Lys cornered by Kareina at the edge of the pit.

"Don't let her spook you Sis!" He screamed. "Remember who you *are!*"

It took a moment for Roger's words to register.

But then, in a flash of insight, Lys realized what Kareina was doing.

The terror I'm feeling... It's from Kareina! She's using her mental powers to call up these memories. She's trying to overwhelm me with fear!

And Lys suddenly knew that her fight was no longer with Kareina. Her struggle was against her own fears. If she allowed Kareina to intimidate her, she would lose. But she didn't have to do that.

Lys was now *restored*. She was fully human! She had every gift the Creator of All Worlds intended her to have. And that meant she had the power to defeat Kareina.

"That's far enough, Kareina," Lys barked. Brushing away her fears, Lys planted her feet, determining not to back up one more inch.

Kareina just laughed and kept advancing.

Then Kareina spread her wings and rose into the air, but Lys activated her life-force and rose also.

Kareina flew in a great circle around Lys, looking for her opportunity to strike.

But Lys was in motion as well, spiraling even higher, her sword shining.

Surprised by Lys's new abilities, Kareina shrieked in rage.

And for the first time in all of their encounters, Kareina dropped her illusion of humanity, becoming what she truly was.

Lys gazed at her foe in disbelief. Kareina was ancient. Her gaunt body was battle-worn and covered with scars. She held her sword firmly in her left hand, but her right arm hung limp, powerless. It suddenly struck Lys that Kareina was one of the smallest Archons she had seen in Hades. Kareina no longer seemed intimidating. She looked weak and frightened and old.

But her fury had not abated. Driven by blind rage, Kareina raised her sword with her good hand and let loose a shuddering roar that shook the depths of Hell. Summoning all of her strength, Kareina held her sword high as she advanced on Lys, her ragged leathery wings beating furiously.

Lys watched her calmly, hovering just above her.

Kareina continued to drive toward Lys, prepared to make a fatal thrust.

Lys extended her sword in response, which was now scintillating with golden light. The atmosphere around her cracked with energy.

As Kareina rose up to strike, Lys pointed her sword directly at Kareina. A single bolt of energy flashed the length of the sword and struck Kareina in the chest.

Confronting Kareina on the Sacred Mountain

Chapter Thirty-Six: After the Comet

STONEHENGE – THE SALISBURY PLAIN, UK

It was over in an instant. The last ones through the portal were Roger and Lys, bringing the thousand captives from the Archon sacred mountain. The last human exited the Stonehenge portal precisely fourteen minutes before Wormwood Beta was due to strike.

Emerging from the portal, Roger and Lys were slammed in the face by a stinging blast of cold, rain-drenched wind, whipping their hair around and making it hard to remain standing. The Wormwood Alpha hurricane had arrived. The sky was now dark and overcast, the great rocks of Stonehenge drenched by an unrelenting downpour. The gale-force wind whistled through the great sarsen stones with an ever-increasing fury.

Seeing that the rescue mission was completed, Erin directed all of the singers to gather around the portal and link their voices as one. Lys and Roger joined them, and the song began to flow out—unlearned words rising in unison from more than 500 singers, mounting in crescendo after crescendo.

Nothing happened. The portal did not expand.

Erin looked on in alarm. The present wormhole was not nearly large enough to encompass the approaching comet. If the wormhole could not be expanded, all of their efforts were in vain.

The hurricane wind continued to intensify. The voices of the singers were now barely audible above the shriek of the storm.

Erin suddenly realized what was happening. *The roar of the storm-wind is drowning out the singers! It's interfering with their ability to extend the portal!*

The comet was due to strike in three minutes. The singers redoubled their efforts, straining their voices, singing with all the strength they could muster. It was an attempt born of sheer desperation. They knew if they did not succeed in enlarging the portal, all life on earth would end within minutes.

Less than two minutes before comet strike, there was a momentary lull in the wind. As the howl of the wind briefly abated, the impassioned song of the singers was at last heard reverberating among the ancient stones.

And in that moment, a shift took place. The portal suddenly began to expand, extending upward and outward, forming a glowing tunnel that burst through the dark clouds overhead.

Wormwood Beta was clearly visible through that tunnel, a brightly glowing sphere directly overhead, steadily increasing in size as it approached.

The synaxis members held their breath.

Would their plan work? Would the earth be spared?

In a brilliant flash of light, Wormwood Beta,

traveling at 132,000 miles an hour, entered the wormhole just above the earth's atmosphere... and vanished.

The moment they were certain the comet was gone, the exhausted singers ceased their song and allowed the portal to close. Many of them collapsed to the soggy ground in exhaustion.

Planet Earth was saved!

Over the next few days, as the comet's tail, composed primarily of microdroplets of water, settled across the earth's upper atmosphere, great rainbows appeared in the sky. They persisted for months afterward. It was a fitting sign that destruction had been averted.

In the realm of Hades, Comet Wormwood Beta, still carrying the old cargo hauler spacecraft and the lifeless body of Belphegor, smashed into the Archon homeworld just above the Great Portal of Abadon. The city of Abadon, its spaceport, the ancient crater, the sacred mountain, and the dreaded arena, were all vaporized in an instant. In that moment, the Archon race ceased to exist.

Michael and Erin hovered above the plain, gazing at the millions of refugees scattered around the Great Portal of Stonehenge. Roger, Jamie, and Marissa had joined them.

The sky remained dark and overcast, the ground drenched by the unrelenting downpour. The Wormwood Alpha storm was now pummeling the ancient Portal with near-hurricane force winds.

All across the Salisbury Plain the newly freed

captives sat huddled in groups to stay warm. Some wore tattered remnants of the clothing they'd been captured in. Some wore the slave smocks they'd been forced to wear in Abadon. Others were naked, wearing nothing at all.

Many were weeping. Some just sat numbly, unsure of what had just happened, and uncertain what the future would hold.

"What are we going to do about these people?" Marissa asked.

"We'll do everything we can, but I know some of them won't make it," Roger said. "But at least they're out of Hades. At least they have a chance."

Patrick and Lys arrived. They'd just flown in a great circle around the sprawling encampment, trying without success to estimate the number of refugees. It was a multitude beyond numbering.

"Holmes just texted that he's organized synaxis groups around the world to send in aid." Patrick said, shouting to be heard over the wind. "He's also alerted the military. While the civilian infrastructure is in shambles right now, the military has promised to send help, though it may take days to arrive."

"I believe conditions will improve rapidly," Roger said. "When the world realizes that destruction has been averted, some level of civilization should be quickly restored. And remember, the evil influence of the Archons has now been removed from our world."

An hour later, swarms of Irin arrived. Hundreds of thousands of them had come pouring through the Iona portal, loaded down with food and supplies. Shelters were erected and hot food prepared. The hurricane was already diminishing.

The next week was one of non-stop activity. With the hurricane's passing, Patrick and Lys worked to supervise the aid distribution. Roger and Marissa partnered with several local physicians to set up emergency treatment centers.

Erin and Sylvia devoted almost all of their time to bringing restoration to other synaxis groups. As the number of restored humans swelled, their ability to deal with the worldwide crises improved.

IONA HOUSE – THE ISLAND OF IONA

At the end of two weeks, Erin and Michael returned to Iona House for a much needed rest.

Without the continual upward pressure provided by the movers, the island of Iona was slowly easing back to its original level. Its surface was continually trembling with minor earthquakes, but it was now less than 100 feet above its normal elevation, and was expected to equalize less than ten feet above its original position. The ferry to Mull would soon be running again.

Relaxing in his recliner in their personal quarters, Michael felt numb. "Being restored doesn't mean you don't get tired," he said wearily.

"But we did it, Michael," Erin answered with a sigh. "We saved Iona. We saved the world!"

She thought back over the past few weeks. It all seemed unreal, like a nightmare she'd be glad to wake up from. But it *was* real. And the task of rebuilding had already begun. The refugee encampment on the Salisbury Plain was rapidly becoming a functioning city.

"Even after such mass disruptions, there's already a surprising level of peace," she said. "I believe the absence of the Archons accounts for a lot of that. When the Archons exited the Earth-realm, their evil influence was removed. As more and more humans are restored, we'll find the world a very different place than anything we've ever known.

"I wonder what it will be like?" Michael mused. "A world without evil. The universe set right."

He remembered the words of the High King. "The Archons brought great evil and much suffering into the universe, but it was necessary to allow them to continue in their way for a time so all the universe could see the true nature of that evil path. But their time is now over. It's time for the universe to be corrected."

The universe corrected. That will be something to see!

Pondering all that had happened since they'd gone to Hi-Ouranos, Michael sat in silence for a long time.

Finally Erin interrupted his reverie. "Michael, is something the matter?"

"What do you mean?"

"You're being so quiet. And it's not just your silence right now. You've been uncharacteristically silent ever since we got back from Hi-Ouranos."

"I've been thinking," he replied, "thinking about a lot of things.

"Mostly I've been thinking about our time in Hi-Ouranos. About the Creator of all Worlds, about the Presence, and especially about the High King."

He was quiet for a moment, then spoke. "It's so strange, Erin. The first time the High King looked at me, I realized that he knew me. What was even more surprising... I sensed that I knew him also. In fact, I felt I'd known him for a very long time. But it wasn't until sometime later that I realized why."

Michael paused again, looking pensive.

"What is it?" Erin prodded.

"You didn't see them did you?"

"See *what?*"

"The High King's hands."

"His *hands?*" Erin said, tilting her head slightly to the left.

"When you knelt before him and he put his hands on your head to activate your gift. I saw his hands. I was shaken to the core."

"What did you see?"

"On the palms of his hands..." Michael responded. "There were very distinctive scars. They appeared to be puncture wounds—like each of his hands had been pierced by a sharply-pointed object."

"I knew immediately what they were. There's really nothing else they could have been.

"They were nail prints."

EPILOGUE

Birthday Party

ALDEBARAN SEVEN – INFORMALLY KNOWN AS "NEW IONA" – 471 YEARS AFTER THE RESTORATION

It was Lys's 500th birthday. Though a 500th birthday was no longer an unusual event, it still felt significant. The whole synaxis had thrown a big party and even baked a gigantic cake for her. Following standard procedure, they'd not added any new candles after the first one hundred.

Lys and Patrick had broken away from the crowd and come out to the broad deck of their home. It was a beautiful evening. The sun hung low in the sky. (They still called the bright orb in the sky 'the sun,' even though it was larger and redder, and clearly *not* the sun. Old habits die hard.) A pleasant breeze was blowing in softly from the Sea of Dreams.

The first stars of night were just appearing. Lys and Patrick loved to sit on the deck in the evenings and think up names for the new constellations. Even after all this time they still had not agreed on names for all of them. There was New Orion, who had four stars in his belt instead of three. There was The Soaring Angel, with large wings spreading out to each side. There was The Archon Warrior, with two blazing red eyes. Lys's favorite object in the sky was not actually a constellation. It was a stunning globular cluster of stars occupying the space the big dipper had held on earth. She called it the Giant Snowball.

"New heavens and a new earth," Patrick mused. "It's all new."

"I sometimes miss looking up and seeing the old constellations," Lys responded, feeling nostalgic. "The Big Dipper. Old Orion. The Pleiades..."

"But you can go back to earth and see them any time you want to," answered Patrick. "Just step through the portal and you're there."

"I know I can, Patrick, but it's not the same. The old constellations aren't something I'd make a special trip just to look at. What I miss is the joy of glancing up and just 'happening' to see them when I *wasn't* looking for them. When I'd glanced up at the sky and see Orion looking down at me, it was like an old friend dropping by unexpectedly.

"I know in time I'll get used to the new constellations, and they'll seem as familiar as the old ones do now. It's just the transition time that seems a little strange."

Their friends had noticed their absence and were gradually filtering out through the French doors to join Patrick and Lys on the deck. Pouring glasses of their favorite wine at the outdoor bar, they all found comfortable seats overlooking the bay.

"Well Orion might not be in the sky, but you have no shortage of old friends today!" Patrick smiled.

Family members had just finished feeding the kids and were now herding them out to the deck as well.

Over the last century, most of the Iona synaxis had re-settled on New Iona, which with children and grandchildren down several generations, meant that New Iona already had a healthy population. Since the restoration, the synaxis no longer really functioned as a synaxis, but they were still family. They enjoyed being together.

In the years after the restoration, the human population of Planet Earth had mushroomed. People remained in childbearing years almost forever, and hardly anyone died. As the population seemed about to overwhelm the planet, the High King revealed that portals could be used to travel between worlds as well as between dimensions.

As a result of that revelation, instantaneous travel now took place between worlds thousands of light-years apart. And there were hundreds of millions of habitable worlds in the universe.

And so the Human Race, with its greatly increased lifespan, began to fulfill its destiny of expanding across the galaxy.

When the time came to cut the cake, Lys's offspring, the children, grandchildren, and great grandchildren down several generations clustered around to sing "Happy Birthday." All of Lys's gathered friends joined in, including several members of the original synaxis, along with Eliel, Rand, and Araton. It took Lys three tries to blow out all the candles.

Though a great, great, grandmother many times over, Lys was not an old woman. In fact, she didn't look or feel any older than the day the Iona portal first opened. The Irin assured her that the first signs of physical aging would not become noticeable for more than a hundred thousand years. Her normal expected lifespan was more than two hundred thousand.

One surprising result of the restoration was that people older than about 40 actually seemed to regress in age.

Michael had been in his late fifties when the restoration took place, but now appeared to be in his early forties. His grey hair had turned light brown, and his joints no longer creaked when he got out of bed in the morning

Even Lys and Roger's parents had regained their youth. They'd moved to New Iona to be close to their offspring, and were enjoying their new life tremendously.

Lys's mother was still designing clothing, and had become more creative than ever.

With little need for lawyers, her dad had decided to pursue his life-long dream of running a vineyard. He'd been at it for fifty years now, and had produced some excellent vintages. And of course, he didn't mind that the lower gravity on New Iona had noticeably improved his golf score.

Patrick and Lys had considered having more children. They were certainly young enough, but right now they were enjoying being "empty nesters." They had plenty of time. Maybe in a few hundred years they might consider having more kids.

From a raised platform to the left of the house, they heard a familiar "whoosh" as a whirlwind began to circle in the middle of a ring of standing stones. The portal was opening.

Old friends had been dropping by all day. This time it was Marissa. She was Marissa Stephens now, and was accompanied by her husband Clive. Though it been sixty years since Lys and Patrick had seen Marissa and Clive, they literally did not look a day older.

"I'd heard you finally moved off-planet," Marissa smiled as she walked up to the deck and gave Lys and Patrick big hugs. Clive warmly shook their hands as well.

Marissa glanced around in amazement.

"I love this place. What are you calling it?"

"Its listed name is Aldebaran Seven, but we've been calling it New Iona. We've actually applied for an official name change."

"I like that. Halfway across the galaxy, and you still live on Iona! Talk about Iona rising!

"It even looks a lot like Iona."

The house stood on a slight rise of land above a broad crescent-shaped white-sand beach. To the east, the Sea of Dreams stretched halfway across the planet. To the west, the road led along a gently flowing river through the village, and into the red granite mountains beyond.

"This looks so much like the Bay at the Back of the Ocean!"

Other members of the Iona synaxis crowded

around to greet Clive and Marissa.

"Have you thought of moving off-world?" Lys asked, "We have plenty of room here on New Iona."

"Maybe someday. We've talked about it from time to time, but Clive really loves Scotland. They've completely rebuilt Glasgow now, you know. And since the restoration, life on earth is pretty idyllic too."

As the sun set, fruit, bread, and cheese were brought out, and the adults broke into small groups, visiting, while the children scampered around the lawn chasing the tiny glowing firebirds that came flitting about each evening.

The sky was now a blaze of glory, with the Giant Snowball shining brightly in the north. It was almost time for the kids to go to bed.

"Alright kids," Lys's great-granddaughter Lindy addressed the brood. "It's bed time. Come tell Nana Lys 'happy birthday' one more time."

As they clustered close, a cute seven-year old with steel-blue eyes and light ash-blonde hair looked up at Lys and pleaded, "Nana Lys, tell us the story. Pleeeasse…"

"Again? I've told that story so many times."

"This is a new generation, Lys." Patrick chided, "Every generation needs to know."

Lys glanced at Lindy. "Do you think it's okay? I know it's already getting pretty late."

"But this is a special occasion," Lindy smiled, "and there's no school tomorrow. And besides, they're all sleeping at your house tonight anyhow."

"Okay," Lys agreed. "But… maybe just the

short version."

Seeing the generations of her offspring clustered around her, Lys was overwhelmed with joy.

"Gather around close kids," she said with a gentle smile, her long, ash-blonde hair feathering softly across her shoulders.

"Now be very quiet and I'll tell you the story."

Lys took a deep breath and began. "It all began one night, many, *many*, years ago, when Nana Lys was driving down a narrow, twisting, mountain road in a far off land called Colorado..."

THE END

NOTES

Here is a little background on a few of the names used in the Synaxis Chronicles trilogy:

Irin – Irin is an ancient Hebrew word for angels. It's commonly translated, "watchers."

Archon – Archon is the Greek word for "ruler." In early Christian writings, Archons were considered to be high-level demonic powers who sought to dominate the Earth-realm.

Synaxis – A Greek word meaning "a gathering together." It was the word used by the early church for their secret house-church meetings. In the Synaxis Chronicles, it symbolizes the church as it was intended to be, supernaturally empowered, expanding and multiplying through the earth to drive back the forces of evil.

Basilea – Basilia is the Greek word for *kingdom*. When the Iona Portal was opened, the "Kingdom" was able to be manifested on the earth, driving back the evil forces of the Archons.

Hades – In Greek mythology, Hades was the name of the underworld. The name later became synonymous with the Christian concept of Hell.

Hi-Ouranos – The Greek word for Heaven is *Ouranos*. Hi-Ouranos in the Synaxis Chronicles is the Highest Heaven, the realm above all realms. The descriptions of Hi-Ouranos in Iona Rising are loosely based on the description of the Heavenly sanctuary in Revelation chapters 4-5.

Eliel – A Hebrew name meaning "My God is God."

Araton – In Medieval theology, Araton is one of the ruling angels over the provinces of Heaven.

Kareina – In Babylonian mythology, "Karina" is a female night-spirit. Very nasty.

Botis, - In Medieval Demonology, Botis was a prince of Hell with 60 legions of demons under his command.

Turell – "Turel" is a fallen angel mentioned in the book of Enoch.

Lys and **Syl** – Two of the main characters in Iona Portal. Syl is "Lys" spelled backward, which is appropriate, because the two are exact opposites. No matter how bad things got, Lys never gave way to passivity. She had an unshakable belief that if she kept trying, she could succeed. Syl, on the other hand, had totally embraced hoplessness. She considered it too much effort to try to resist the enemy. The result was that Syl was destroyed while Lys moved forward to fulfill her destiny. The good news is (as we learned in Iona Rising) that the High King had a way for Syl to be restored and fulfill her destiny also.

ABOUT THE AUTHOR

Robert David MacNeil is an author, wine-lover, and student of things supernatural. Over the last twenty years he's traveled to more than 31 nations, writing, and teaching on angels, demons, and supernatural encounters. His travels have taken him from the steppes of Mongolia to the jungles of Thailand, and from the Eskimo villages of Northwest Alaska to *le fin del mundo*, the "end of the world," at the tip of South America.

Long a fan of sci-fi and suspense thrillers, Robert also has a love for history–especially ancient Greece, Rome and medieval Europe. He's particularly fascinated with Patrick, Columba, and the ancient Celts of Ireland and Scotland. The Celtic monks had a special relationship with the angels.

Robert and his wife, Linda, live near Dallas, Texas. He has authored eight non-fiction books under a different name. Robert's novels include Iona Portal, Iona Stronghold, and Iona Rising.

For those curious to know Robert's true identity, Robert David MacNeil is the pen name and fictional persona of Dr. Robert Heidler, a teacher with Glory of Zion International Ministries in Corinth, TX. You can contact Robert and check out his other books at the Glory of Zion website, **www.GloryofZion.org**. You can also visit Robert at **ionaportal.com**

PLEASE HELP SPREAD THE WORD

**If you've enjoyed reading IONA
RISING and the other books of the Synaxis
Chronicles, please tell please your friends.
Independently published books
depend on "word of mouth" publicity.**

**If you'd like to help even more, you can drop
by Amazon.com and leave a nice review!**

Made in the USA
Middletown, DE
13 August 2020